WE MEET AGAIN...

WE MEET AGAIN...

•

Patricia K. Azeltine

AVALON BOOKS
NEW YORK

PRINTED IN THE UNITED STATES OF AMERICA
ON ACID-FREE PAPER
BY HADDON CRAFTSMEN, BLOOMSBURG, PENNSYLVANIA

To my mother, Mary Burian, and my father, Charles John Burian,
and my sisters, Suzanne Goodwin, Denise Burian,
Diane Burian, Debbie Belmore, and Donna Moore for your
support and encouragement. Thank you.

Special thanks to Jean Cothary for your expertise on Shakespeare,
and my mentor, Frank Lambirth for imparting his experience
and vast knowledge to me.

As always, thanks to my husband, Steve, and
my daughters, Mary and Katie.

Chapter One

"**H**elp!" Paige McCormick yelled. "Someone. Anyone. Please. I need help!"

The hot air balloon rose higher. The Butler brothers, owners of the balloon, chased after the dangling ropes that just moments before were secured to stakes in the ground. With a mighty leap, one brother grabbed a rope. Suddenly he crashed into a wooden fence, let the rope slip through his hands, and watched the balloon—and Paige—sail away. They yelled something to her, but she couldn't understand what they were saying.

Within minutes, Paige and the large rainbow balloon reached the east end of the small country town of Patterson, located twenty miles away from the Oregon coast, her course following west on Main Street.

Wondering faces gazed up at her. Some people waved.

"I don't know how to fly this thing!" she cried. The

balloon continued to rise, its vibrant rainbow colors attracting onlookers, but no rescuers.

Paige bit her lower lip, desperately trying to suppress the panic welling up inside, and glanced at the photography equipment at her feet. The thought of taking aerial shots of the town for her book would play second fiddle to her current plight: how to get herself and this balloon safely to the ground. Oh, God. She was going to crash and ruin her equipment, along with a few bones. She would like to keep both intact.

Paige noticed a cord hanging above her head, and reached out to pull it down. The gas burner rumbled and the balloon lifted. Quickly, she released the cord. Bad idea. She didn't want to go higher. She wanted to get down on solid ground.

The basket jiggled as she scooted from one side to the other. She should have known better than to rent a hot air balloon ride from three brothers named Curly, Larry, and Moe. The sign on their barn's roof, *Butler Brothers' Hot Air Balloon Rides. Safe and Reliable,* glared out as if mocking her. Right now, as she floated in the Butler's runaway balloon, Paige would disagree with that advertisement.

The balloon silently drifted down the main street, guided by a gentle breeze. Patterson was a small community with the strangest people Paige had ever met, which was saying a lot, since her job as a photographer had taken her around the world and back. In fact, traveling was all she had done since she'd finished college five years ago. Even though she was growing tired of constantly being on the move, she didn't have any immediate plans of what she wanted to do, or where she wanted to live. She was sure, though, that Patterson would be her last choice. Eighteen years of living here had been enough.

Paige spotted a group of her grandmother's friends strolling away from the church, dressed in their Sunday best. Zoe Bockner led the group, a little old lady who made it her business to know about everyone else's business in town. Beside Zoe stood Lily Fern, who claimed she could communicate with animals, plants, and even the dead. Dawdling behind the first two ladies were Jean Welsh and Vivian Perish.

"Jean!" Paige cried. "Get help."

Jean's mouth moved. Paige couldn't hear what she said, but knew that most likely whatever passed between Jean's lips was a quote from Shakespeare. Jean loved Shakespeare, and her home reflected it, with dolls dressed in costumes from *Macbeth, Hamlet,* and *The Tempest,* and books and pictures all related to the famous playwright. The ladies continued on their way, oblivious to Paige's current predicament.

Because her grandmother lived here, Paige visited Patterson twice a year. And that was the only reason Paige returned. Granny, eccentric as the rest of the town, making moonshine and immersed in the town history, fit right in.

Now, Granny needed her help.

Since the death of her husband eighteen months ago, Granny's life had revolved around living rent-free in a studio apartment and running the town museum, both located in the Taylor mansion.

The new owner of the mansion would be coming any day to evict Granny—and the museum. Paige hoped to help Granny out while Paige finished her latest photography book on small towns across America.

Further down the street, Paige noticed Patterson's mayor and yelled, "Mr. Gunthrey. Help me."

Fredrick Gunthrey, wearing a red and black plaid shirt

with red suspenders, pushed out of his wooden chair in front of the weather-worn brick Town Hall. He reminded Paige of Santa Claus with his white hair, round cheeks, and large stomach. This man needed no padding when he played Santa Claus each December. Mr. Gunthrey shielded his eyes from the bright fall sunshine, waved, then returned to his chair to resume his intense checker game with the town barber, Barney Dowell. Except during the harsh winter months, Fred and Barney played checkers every Sunday in the same spot at noon, and had for the last twenty years. Notches on the posts out front recorded their wins and loses.

Paige sighed. If she intended to get down, she would have to do it herself. The hot air would eventually run out, right? So she had nothing to worry about. Unless . . . she crashed into a tree, or building. . . . Paige grabbed hold of the basket rim, her hands clenched so tight her white knuckles showed. She bet her face was as white. Not often would she admit it, but right now, she was scared. She didn't know how to operate the balloon, leaving her feeling vulnerable, something she didn't like.

Paige spotted the Butler brothers' pickup truck, speeding down Main Street. At least they were coming after her. She started to relax when they took a turn in the opposite direction from her. They parked in front of a local tavern. They couldn't have lost her location. The balloon stood out like a sore thumb.

Her eyes widened as the brothers stopped to chat with a group of men out front. What were they doing? She was floating alone in their runaway balloon, and they stop to shoot the breeze!

Nearing the edge of town, she drifted closer to the Taylor mansion. The grand Victorian structure, modernized in white paint and brick red shingles, boasted thirty-two rooms, rounded bay windows, brick chimneys, a second-story veranda balcony that, like the main front porch, ran the length of the exterior, and was held up by large, ornately decorated beams. But the mansion's most impressive feature was its third-floor glass dome that consumed much of the roof. Intricate latticework covered the base of the house, much of it hidden by the overgrown shrubs and trees. A cobblestone driveway wound around the front of the home and encircled a ceramic fountain that no longer spouted water.

The conservatory, located at the east end and surrounded on two sides by tall fir trees, housed the Patterson museum, Granny's pride and joy.

Paige's grandfather had donated a valuable family heirloom to it: a gold urn. The urn had been given to Paige's great-great-great-(well, she wasn't sure how many greats) grandfather, Addison McCormick, by George Washington himself. Addison had been a spy for General Washington, and had carried a secret message in the urn, or so the story went. Knowing her family, they had embellished the tale, adding to it throughout the generations.

Nevertheless, the town was proud of its founding settlers, and Paige was proud of her ancestor. The only time the urn hadn't been on display at the museum was when Paige's grandfather passed away, and her grandmother had placed his ashes inside. But since then it remained safely inside a locked display case.

Floating above the mansion, Paige caught sight of a figure, clad in black from head to toe, sneaking out the museum's back door, and carrying something heavy. A flash of light gleamed as the sun caught the object at just the right angle. Paige shaded her eyes with her hands, squinting to get a better look.

The urn!

"Stop. Thief!" Someone was stealing her family's heirloom. She had to get help. Unfortunately, this end of Patterson appeared as deserted as a tomb.

The figure, hunched over and lugging the heavy urn, waddled up a knoll, and then disappeared into the thicket of the evergreens behind the museum.

Paige glanced ahead. Fields of checkered farmland stretched as far as the eye could see, with only a few houses scattered here and there.

Feeling helpless, Paige could only watch as a handful of townspeople drove their cars in and out of Patterson, all oblivious to the fact that the museum had just been robbed.

Paige sailed out of town, letting the balloon gently descend. She surveyed the terrain. The area was beautiful, if one liked rolling green pastures, brilliant blue sky, a bright yellow sun, and clean, crisp air. Not her. She preferred the hustle and bustle of the city, paved streets, and the convenience of a variety of stores to meet her every need.

Many farmers in Patterson raised dairy cows, producing the milk, butter, cheese, and ice cream that were the economic vitality of the town. Spotting a lone farmer on a sloping hill, Paige's hopes mounted. If she was lucky, the ropes would be within his reach. "Hey, mister! Can you help me? I'm in a runaway balloon."

He whirled towards her, his startled look replaced by one of earnestness. Shifting into action with grace and ease, he positioned himself to grasp the rope. Just as he reached out, the rope wiggled away. He didn't give up, chasing after it.

This man was Paige's only chance to get down safely.

She had no time to lose. If she didn't get to the sheriff's office soon, the urn would be long gone.

Focusing back on her rescuer, she said, "You almost had it." He was the first person to come to her aid. Heck, he was the first person to even hear her. And where were those Butler brothers? She thought they would have resumed the chase by now.

The stranger now had a firm hold of the rope with both hands. Suddenly, he took flight.

Scouting ahead, Paige saw a barn blocking his path. If he didn't do something quickly, he would crash into the wall.

"Climb the rope," Paige urged. She leaned over the basket, clinging tightly with one hand to the rim.

"I'm—trying—to," he gasped.

The power in his muscular forearms drew her attention to his broad shoulders as he clambered up, his feet squeezing the rope beneath. The appreciation of his fine physical shape flooded her with warmth, and reddened her cheeks. Shaking off the feeling, Paige extended her arm. "Take my hand."

"I'll grab the basket," he said. She stared at the strong, pliant fingers wrapped around the rim. In the next instant, he kicked one leg into the gondola, followed by the other. Just as he steadied on both feet, the dangling ropes whipped against a barn. He hauled the long ropes in, dropping them on the floor of the basket.

Paige squeezed her fists, resisting the urge to throw her arms around this tall, handsome stranger and thank him profusely with kisses. She had never been so frightened in her entire life. With her luck, she would have ended up in another state before the balloon ran out of hot air. "Please, get me down—"

"Garrett," he clipped, gazing up at the balloon.

"What?" Paige asked.

"My name's Garrett."

"Oh, sorry. I'm Paige McCormick. Do you know how to fly one of these things?"

"Nope."

"No? How are we going to get down?" Her tone came out far shriller than she intended.

He wrapped his fingers around the cord that ignited the flame.

"Don't pull it," Paige said.

He tugged on the cord. The balloon gently ascended.

"What did you do that for? I want to go down, not up."

He nodded for her to turn and look ahead. "Because we'll crash into that tree if we don't."

Minutes later, maple tree branches covered in leaves of brilliant golds, reds, and oranges scraped the bottom of the basket, jostling it. Paige teetered back, then fell forward, finding herself suddenly in Garrett's arms. His body felt warm, inviting and safe. She gazed into his face and his breath brushed her cheek. She had never believed in love at first sight, but right now, her heart was telling her it did indeed exist.

"Are you okay?" he asked.

Paige didn't want to move away, and for a moment, she continued to stare into his eyes, their deep blue drawing her into their depths. His black hair—cut short and neatly groomed as if to control unruly curls—shimmered with the sun's light. The brilliant white of his smile contrasted nicely with his bronzed skin. His jaw—square and firm— spoke of determined purpose, his mouth well-shaped and solemn, yet sensual. He smelled pleasantly of aftershave. Too pleasantly. . . .

Her pulse fluttered.

Slightly dizzy, Paige stepped back. She wasn't sure why she reacted to this particular man, and she didn't want to know. Her job kept her on the go, which left no time for long-distance relationships. And that was the way she liked it.

No involvement.

No complications.

No problems.

Yet . . . Garrett was such an undeniably handsome man, one she could so easily fall for. Maybe it was time to let go and allow herself to fall head over heels in love. Just looking at Garrett, gazing into his eyes, she knew it wouldn't take much.

"I'm, uh, fine." She shuffled several inches back, bumping into the side of the gondola, and then quickly turned her attention to the matter at hand. "How do we get down from here?"

"First, I think we need to find a good place to land," Garrett said.

"I think you're right." Paige caught a glance of Garrett's profile. The smooth lines of his face, and the slant of his jaw looked familiar. Suddenly, the muscles in her shoulders tensed. She looked quickly away, pretending to search for a landing spot. With as much composure as she could collect she said, "What's your last name, Garrett?"

"Taylor. Garrett Taylor."

Paige clamped her lips together to hold back a gasp. She felt as if someone had struck her in the stomach with an iron fist. Breathlessly, she asked, "As in the new owner of the Taylor mansion?"

"Yes." He didn't look at her when he spoke. "But not for long, I hope."

A thick silence filled the spaced between them. Paige wanted to jump overboard, and would have too, if she hadn't been so afraid of heights—and breaking every bone in her body.

"You're evicting my grandmother, and putting the museum out of business." The words spilled from her mouth before she could stop herself. That happened every time she became upset.

He tilted his head and studied her as if confused by her reaction. "I know."

Paige grimaced, trying to quell the rising irritation. He held all the cards and he knew it. Somehow she had to turn the tables around or Granny and the museum would be evicted in the blink of an eye.

Could she appeal to his sense of compassion? Anything was worth a try.

"You're throwing a little old, helpless grandmother out on the street. The museum draws tourists from all over the country to Patterson. Without it, the town will die, and so will my poor grandmother from a broken heart!" Okay, that was a bit exaggerated. So what if the museum looked more like an abandoned building than a flourishing tourist spot? He didn't have to know that.

Garrett burst out laughing. "You haven't changed since our school days."

Paige hadn't anticipated that response. Plus, the last thing she wanted to talk or think about were the 'good old days.' She had tried to erase those painful times from her memory long ago.

"That was years ago," Paige said.

"Not that long ago. Don't try and con me."

The man hit a direct blow. He couldn't have hurt her more if he had used a gun, knife, or club. All her life she had been ashamed of her father's reputation, and her mother's constant denial of what he was doing. That's why Paige had moved across the country, to Chicago. She didn't want anyone finding out about her father's "mistakes," because the second they did, she would be labeled the same: a con, a thief, a swindler. Or worse, they would give her that look of pity, while clutching tighter to their purse or wallet.

Why did she have to pay for the sins of her father?

She forced back a shudder, as the memories of growing up in Patterson rushed to mind. It had been horrible. She'd had few, if any, friends. No one had given her a chance. So she had become tough on the outside, and kept mostly to herself. She couldn't remember a time while growing up when she hadn't carried a chip on her shoulder—a "bad attitude," her teachers used to say.

Her father might have gone to prison for stealing and cheating people out of money, but she wasn't like him. From the time she was a small child, she had vowed to be just the opposite: honest and forthright. But she had learned at an early age that most people automatically labeled her. How many times had she been accused of stealing something?

Maybe that's why she lived like a gypsy, moving around, choosing a career that never kept her in one place for very long. That way, no one could ever get too close to her, and find out her dark secret about her family's past.

Paige briefly closed her eyes against the onslaught of resentment. Garrett had had it all. Rich parents, smartest kid in school, the best athlete, and girls falling all over him. He had done everything perfectly. Even time hadn't diminished his looks. Everyone loved Garrett and always had since the first day of school. He had had more friends than Paige could count.

Which made her wonder, why had he moved away?

"If you knew it was me, then why did you help?" She sounded deflated, like she wished this balloon was.

"I guess I'm a sucker for a damsel in distress." Garrett smiled, met her glance, then looked away. He tapped a dial attached to the inside of the gondola. "The altimeter is broken," he said, as if trying to change the subject. "But the pyrometer and the variometer are working."

He might as well be talking Greek. She didn't have a clue what all those meter things did, and she could care less. She just wanted to land the balloon safely—and the sooner the better.

Paige had a robbery to report! The urn, that precious hunk of metal that gave her family just a little bit of credibility, just a tiny bit of respect, had just been stolen. Paige wanted it back. Every second that ticked by gave the thief that much of a head start.

Paige made an impatient gesture. "Could you please get us down?"

"What's the hurry? Look at the view."

"This isn't a joyride for me. I had intended to take aerial shots of the town for my book. But something more important's come up."

"Book? You wrote a book?" He sounded genuinely impressed.

"I have a series of books. I'm a photographer."

He raised his brows, but said nothing other than, "All right then, down we go." Reaching up, he pulled on a cord to release some hot air. The balloon slowly sank. "This looks like a safe place to land." A flat, tilled field sprawled before them. In the summer it would grow corn, wheat, or hay. Now it was just clumps of churned-up dirt.

"I thought you said you didn't know how to fly one of these things," Paige said.

Garrett's grin was lazy, insolent. "I've ridden in them a few times, but I'm not licensed to fly one."

A few times, her foot. He knew exactly what he was doing, maneuvering the huge rainbow bubble gently down. Paige gripped the sides, holding on tightly.

The gondola jolted when they hit the ground, then skidded for several feet before coming to a stop.

Her tone icy, Paige said, "I suppose you were hoping to whisk me out of town before I could con anyone out of their money?"

Just once couldn't someone, anyone, see her for the person she really was—hard working, reliable, caring . . . and honest?

"Maybe I wanted to talk to you."

"What would we possibly have to talk about, Garrett? We come from opposite sides of the fence."

"Maybe when we were kids, but not now."

"Oh, no? What about my grandmother and the museum?" She rushed on before he could reply. "I'm warning you. I'll do whatever it takes to help her." Her brown eyes locked on his abruptly, directly, and defiantly.

He held the stare. "I'll remember that."

Paige climbed out of the gondola. "You do that."

As Garrett began the process of deflating the balloon, the Butler brothers' truck pulled up and screeched to a halt. A plume of dust floated towards Paige and Garrett.

Paige coughed and sputtered, waving at the dust. The Butlers barely took a step out of their beat-up old truck before Paige descended on them.

"It's about time you guys showed up. You three did nothing to get me down safely. Instead, a total stranger helped me. I should sue you and your lousy balloon business!"

Larry slid the hat off his balding head. "Uh . . . we're sorry about that, Miss."

"This has never happened to us before," Curly added.

"We didn't know what to do," Moe said. "We were real worried about you, though."

Paige folded her arms over her chest. "So worried you stopped off at the tavern to have a friendly visit with the locals?"

Larry and Curly scurried over to the balloon and took over for Garrett.

"Now, Miss. We were getting advice from Tommy Joe Potts. He's flown balloons for nearly forty years. By the time we got what we needed from the hardware store, you had landed. We had a heck of a time finding you."

Garrett joined them, carrying Paige's camera equipment. "No harm was done."

"What about mental anguish?" she said, half sarcastically, half seriously. She lifted her equipment bag from Garrett's hand and positioned the strap over her shoulder.

"Look, if there's anything we can do to make it up to you—how about the next balloon ride's free?" Moe offered.

Paige produced a hard, brittle laugh. "I'll pass. What I need is a ride into town."

Moe quickly said, "We'd be glad to drive you after we take care of the balloon."

"I can't wait," Paige glanced at the nearby farmhouse. "Do you know someone in the area who could give me a ride?"

"I know someone," Garrett said. "Come on." He nudged her arm, then started out, walking across the plowed field.

"Who?" Paige asked.

"The man who's renting that place." He pointed to the farmhouse across the field. "I'm sure if you ask nicely he'll give you a ride."

"Just as long as he doesn't have an out-of-control car to take me in. I've beat fate once today. I might not be so lucky a second time," Paige said.

Garrett grinned, but said nothing.

Paige had to jog just to keep up with Garrett's long strides. He made no attempt to slow down. Breathlessly, she asked, "What's his name?"

"Garrett Taylor."

Paige groaned inwardly. Lucky her. Now she couldn't get away from him. To be truthful, she wanted to run away from Garrett, run away from anyone who knew her, and most of all, run away from her past and all the pain that came with it. Timbuktu wouldn't be far enough.

She opened her mouth to turn his offer down, but she couldn't think of one good reason not to take him up on it. Besides, she needed to see the sheriff, and walking would take too long.

"I don't know. That'll give you another chance to whisk me out of town."

He chuckled, and then winked at her.

Paige wondered if he thought what she had said was funny, or he laughed because she had read his thoughts. They completed the rest of their journey silence. Paige walked directly to the passenger's side of a black 1940s Ford truck, the only vehicle in sight. "Are we taking this car?"

"We'll have to since my other car is still at the dairy

farm." Garrett climbed into the driver's seat and ignited the engine. The truck purred like a contented kitten.

Paige slipped into the passenger's side and shut the door. "The car sounds great for its age."

Garrett smiled. "I've been working on it."

"I remember when I was a little girl seeing your grandfather drive around town in this. It was old even then." Everything in Patterson was old, the homes, the cars—and the majority of the population.

Paige had liked Garrett's grandfather. He had been kind and treated everyone like an equal, despite his vast wealth. Of course, if she hadn't known Rocky, as he was nicknamed, she never would have guessed he'd had money. The man had always dressed in jean overalls, a flannel or T-shirt, depending on the weather, and worn boots.

"He loved this car. This was the first automobile my grandfather ever bought brand new. He called it Bertha when it was running well, and other names when it wasn't." Garrett's eyes glistened. He blinked several times, then turned his head away to stare out his side window.

"What were you doing at a dairy farm, before you rescued me?" Okay, so she was a little curious about him, that's all. He was probably married and had a dozen kids by now.

"I was checking on one of the Hanson's sick cows."

"When did you learn about cows?" she asked in surprise.

"When I became a veterinarian."

"I don't remember you even liking animals." Her gaze followed the perfect lines of his profile, the classically sculpted nose and square chin that spoke of a stubborn will.

He smiled that sexy smile that transformed his face. "You noticed me back then, huh?"

Who hadn't? And who wouldn't notice him now? He

had gotten even better with age. "Maybe a little." Paige glanced down quickly, feeling heat rise in her cheeks.

He sobered. "I liked animals. My father just wouldn't allow them." He returned his attention back to the road. A muscle flexed along his jaw.

A hush settled inside the cab of the truck until they reached the edge of town.

"Where can I take you?" Garrett asked.

"To the sheriff's office."

"The sheriff's office. Why?" Garrett sounded alarmed. His expression said the same. "You're not bailing out a family member, are you?"

Not funny. Paige gave him a cool look. She didn't dignify his smart-aleck comment with an answer as she climbed out of the car. The last thing she wanted him to know was that his precious mansion had been broken into. He would undoubtedly blame it on the McCormicks.

"Thanks for the ride and for getting the balloon down." She shut the door quickly before he could respond. She could feel his stare on her until she closed the sheriff's office door behind her.

Paige had seen the inside of the Patterson sheriff's office a time or two before, bailing out her father, but that had been years ago. The old brick building hadn't changed a bit. The small office still had three jail cells, two desks, several file cabinets, and a gun case. Even Deputy Dave and Sheriff Raymond were still working there, but now their dark hair had faded to gray. Sheriff Raymond's stomach hung over his belt, while Deputy Dave had grown skeleton thin. Wrinkles flourished around their eyes, mouth, and on their foreheads. Deputy Dave was old then. Now he must be ancient.

"What can I do for you?" Sheriff Raymond asked.

Paige took a deep breath before blurting out. "I want to report a theft."

Deputy Dave looked ready to nod off, his head drooping lower and lower. This jerked him awake. "A theft?" he asked, his eyes widening beyond thin slits, his voice old and crackly. "I'll nab the critter." Pushing out of his chair, he retrieved his gun belt from the hook on the wall.

"Critter?" Paige said, shaking her head. "It wasn't an animal. I saw a person."

Sheriff Raymond held his hand up, signaling Deputy Dave to slow down. He took out a pad and pen. "Let me get your name, then tell me exactly what you saw?"

"My name's Paige McCormick." A dead silence filled the room, just as she expected, and the two men exchanged glances.

"Little Paige McCormick! Why I haven't seen you in years. How's your mother doing?" Sheriff Raymond asked.

"Fine, but I didn't come here to chat. A crime has been committed. We need to move on this immediately."

As if she hadn't said a word, Deputy Dave said, "I heard she'd remarried and moved to Arizona."

Paige rolled her eyes. "Yes, she did."

"Your father out of jail now?"

"He's been out of jail for ten years."

"How long was he in for?" Deputy Dave asked.

Through gritted teeth, she said, "Two years. He got out early on good behavior."

"You come back to town to live with your grandma?" Sheriff Raymond asked.

"Sheriff," she said in a curt tone, "I've come here to report a crime. Are you interested in hearing about it or not?"

"Boy, you're sure testy, aren't you?" Deputy Dave mumbled. He moseyed back to his seat, and plopped down. "Got a little of your grandmother in you, I'd say."

"All right, all right," Sheriff Raymond said. "Why don't you tell us what you saw?"

Finally. "I was riding in a hot air balloon, taking aerial photos of the town. When the balloon floated at the end of Main Street, I saw someone run out the back entrance of the museum with my family's urn in his hands."

"Then it was a man?" Deputy Dave asked.

Paige hesitated. "I think it was. It was hard to tell. I was drifting pretty high up in the balloon, and everything happened so fast."

Sheriff Raymond tapped his pen on the paper. "What was this alleged thief wearing?"

"Black clothes from head to toe."

Deputy Dave folded his bony hands on his desk. "Are you sure he stole the urn?"

"Today's Sunday. The museum's closed."

"Why don't we go take a look and see if anything's missing?" Sheriff Raymond asked, as if trying to placate her.

Fine. He could be as condescending as he wanted. Paige didn't care. All that mattered was finding the thief and getting the urn back.

Paige led the way out the door. On foot, they crossed the street. The trek took forever with Deputy Dave trailing along. His old, spindly legs didn't carry him as fast as they used to.

They headed up the long driveway to the front of the house, then proceeded directly to the conservatory. Despite the conservatory having large windows on three sides, the interior was dark due to the shade from the huge cedar trees outside, and the lack of interior lights.

"You stay here just in case someone's still in there," Sheriff Raymond said to Paige. "I'll check the door to the museum around the back. Dave can check the doors to the mansion and see if he can get in the museum from inside the house."

"But I saw the thief exit out the back. I don't think anyone's in there," Paige said.

"That's the difference between a private citizen and a trained professional," Deputy Dave said, tapping his finger to his head. "We know how to handle situations like this."

Paige wasn't too sure about that. She watched from a distance.

Sheriff Raymond rounded the museum, and peered in a window, before disappearing behind a sprawling, leafy bush. Deputy Dave set on foot in the opposite direction, rattling locked door handles and checking windows. Soon he vanished around the side of the house.

Sheriff Raymond returned first. "Looks like you're right. The museum's been broken into."

"What about the urn?" Paige hoped and prayed she had been mistaken.

"It's gone." The sheriff sounded apologetic. "The museum's never been robbed before." He scratched his head as if he didn't know what to do. "Where's your grandma?"

"Visiting her sister in Twilling," Paige said. "She should be back within the hour."

"I guess the only thing to do then is to call Garrett Taylor and tell him the bad news," the sheriff said.

"You can't." Oops. The words slipped out before she could stop herself. "He's already trying to evict Granny and the museum. This will only give him ammunition to toss her and the town's history out even faster."

A sympathetic expression puckered the sheriff's face.

"Your grandma's worked real hard to help out at the museum." He shrugged. "But I have to. Garrett Taylor owns the place."

Paige's shoulders slumped. She would be lucky if Garrett gave them a day to get everything out before he kicked them out into the street. She sighed.

The sheriff waited with Paige until Deputy Dave ambled over and joined them. "Good news. It looks as if nothing else was taken and the burglar's long gone," Deputy Dave said.

A crash came from inside the main house.

Chapter Two

Paige exchanged alarming glances with the sheriff and Deputy Dave. "I sure hope that wasn't the ghost Granny said she's been hearing in the house lately."

"Ghost?" Deputy Dave asked.

"Yes. Haunting the house," Paige said.

"Ghost or no ghost, we need to investigate," Sheriff Raymond said. He lowered his voice to a whisper. "It sounded like the noise came from the room by the front door." He drew his gun, and motioned for Paige to stay put. The deputy followed.

A few townspeople began to gather halfway up the driveway. The break-in was probably more excitement than this town had seen in years.

While the sheriff rounded the back of the house, Deputy Dave approached the home's grand entryway. The doors were beautifully crafted with inlaid stained-glass panels of roses.

The deputy twisted the handle again, finding it locked. Then, using his shoulder, he threw his body against the door, rebounding off and stumbling backward.

Paige wanted to close her eyes and not watch this old, brittle-boned man attempt to break down a heavy hand-carved wooden door. In this contest, she knew his bones would be the first to go.

This time, Dave gave himself a shuffling start. Just as he reached the front door, at full speed, it opened. Unable to stop himself, the deputy crashed into the house. A loud clatter followed. After a minute, Sheriff Raymond appeared at the door, raised one hand and said, "Deputy Dave is fine." He motioned for Paige.

She hastened inside the house and immediately spotted her cat, Buster, slinking away from the vase with fragments scattered on the hardwood floor in the parlor. The white, fluffy Persian feline had a nasty habit of breaking things, usually valuable things, which was how he got his name.

"Do you know who owns this cat?" Sheriff Raymond asked.

"I do. Here kitty, kitty, kitty." Buster inched over to her, taking his sweet time. Scooping him up, Paige held him in her arms. "Bad kitty. You broke Mr. Taylor's vase." Buster rubbed his head on her shoulder, bringing a smile to her lips. She never could stay mad at Buster. He was her best friend and went everywhere with her. "I'd better take you back to Granny's. I don't know how you got inside."

"I guess our work is done here," Sheriff Raymond said.

Deputy Dave joined them, dragged in a deep breath, yanked up his sagging pants by the waistband, and exhaled on a sigh. "Guess we scared the burglar right out of the house."

"The burglar wasn't in the house," Sheriff Raymond said. "The cat broke the vase."

"Maybe that's exactly what the burglar wants us to think." Deputy Dave nodded his head as if he had it all figured out.

Sheriff Raymond shook his head. "Come on. Let's get back to the station and fill out a report on the stolen urn."

Garrett brought his truck to a screeching halt, jumped out, then slammed the door behind him. He charged over to where Paige sat, on the mansions top porch step, and glared at her. "Okay, which one of your relatives broke in?"

As she stood, her hands automatically fisted at her side. "How dare you?"

He wished he could take those words back, but it was too late, his temper had gotten the better of him.

Her lips, squeezed together in outrage, were full, seductive. She had a stubborn streak in her, just like her grandmother. The very thought challenged him. Resisting the urge to comfort her, he shoved his hands in the front pockets of his jeans. Paige probably wouldn't accept help from anyone in this town, especially him. He didn't blame her.

"Sorry," he mumbled. His gaze moved to the mansion. "What was taken?"

"Don't worry. None of the precious Taylor possessions are missing. The only thing stolen was my family's urn." She swallowed as if to rid herself of a lump in her throat. "I suppose you'll want Granny to move out even sooner now."

"She'll survive. She always does." Paige was a survivor too. That's what Garrett had always admired about her, her ability to continue on, no matter the odds, no matter how difficult the situation. She was strong—and so damn beautiful!

"How? I travel the globe in my job. I can't take care of her." Paige folded her arms over her chest as if to ward off any further insults he would throw at her.

"Your grandmother makes a living making moonshine. And, from what I understand, she makes good money at it."

"It's tonic. For medicinal purposes."

"Yeah, it can cure just about anything for a few hours."

She raised her shoulder and hands. A smile curved her lips, changing her face from beautiful to gorgeous. "See, it works."

Garrett grinned. A fighter. Yes, definitely a fighter. Paige was unlike any other woman he had ever met, and he'd met plenty—tall, short, successful, struggling, young, mature—but they all seemed to be missing that key ingredient, that spark that got his blood boiling.

He pulled a key out of his jeans pocket, hopped up the steps, crossed the broad porch, and then found the front door unlocked. He thought it best to double-check, just to make sure nothing was damaged or missing.

He pushed the door wide, pausing on the threshold. Garrett hadn't been in this house since his grandfather's funeral, and had managed to avoid coming here since arriving in Patterson a week ago.

So many emotions confronted him. His heart felt heavy as an all-consuming emptiness filled him. Why hadn't this feeling of loss lightened over the months? His grandfather had passed away well over a year ago. When would it get easier?

The main house hadn't been used since his grandfather had moved into a rest home only months before his death.

Garrett was grateful that Paige followed him inside. This was not a time when he wanted to be alone. Especially with the flood of memories pressing in on him right now. Most of the memories were good—his grandfather reading to him while they sat together in his rocking chair, a warm crackling fire blazing in the hearth, and the smell of his grandmother's chocolate chip cookies baking in the oven, made just for him. He had thanked God many times for his grandparents.

Despite the musty smell, Garrett could still detect the faint odor of roses his grandmother had always kept in the house, and his grandfather had continued to keep after she had passed away. The aroma had always made his grandfather feel as if she were still around, a way to trick his mind into forgetting the deep pain of a loved one no longer there.

White sheets covered most of the furniture, and a few spider webs hung in the corners of the rooms and doorways. He glanced into the parlor. His stare zeroed in on his grandfather's chair, the brown, velvety fabric worn and faded from years of use.

How Garrett had loved that man!

Rocky had never judged people. Loving him had been so easy for Garrett, much easier than loving his own father. Garrett shook his head to rid himself of the thought.

Breaking out of his reverie, Garrett said, "Looks like someone came in here too." He stepped over to the bits and pieces of vase on the floor.

"Oh. My cat did that. Sorry. I'll pay for the damage." Her explanation was met with silence. "Your home is beautiful," Paige said.

His home. The idea made him uncomfortable. This had been, and would always be, his grandfather's home. Not his. He didn't deserve this house. He hadn't done anything during his life to earn the mansion. But sadly, he had been the only grandchild to pass it on to.

During his grandfather's absence, the place had lapsed into disrepair. Out front, the yard looked like a jungle, with overgrown shrubs, knee-deep grass, and weeds flourishing in the flowerbeds. Quite a contrast to the manicured grounds of years past.

And since he had no intention of staying in Patterson, and no reason to keep the mansion, he knew the best thing to do would be to sell it.

Who was he kidding? He wanted to sell the place, move his mother out of this town, and keep his family's past a secret.

Garrett's tone came out more gruffly than he had intended. "It's not my house. It's my grandfather's."

Paige studied him. He had a hard time meeting her dark brown eyes that, at the moment, seemed to be looking right through him.

"Your grandfather gave you his home. He wanted you to have it. You should be grateful." She strolled past him and into the parlor.

Garrett followed her with his stare. She sure had turned into a beautiful woman. He remembered her as a scrawny teenager, who kept her hair cut short, like a boy's, and wore baggy jeans with holes in the knees, and oversized T-shirts. Now, she still wore jeans, but they fit her snugly; her hair was silky long; and instead of a T-shirt she wore a red sweatshirt.

Paige whirled around and caught him looking her over. A smile curved her lips, but he wasn't sure if it was a smile of disgust or pleasure. He hoped it was the latter.

"I don't know how you could possibly think of selling

this house. This is your heritage. Everything of your grand-father's is in here." She shivered. "It's almost as if you can feel his presence. Granny said she's been hearing him roam the mansion recently."

Garrett shrugged. He didn't feel any supernatural pres-ence, and he didn't believe in such things.

"The mansion's in better hands with a developer," Gar-rett said.

She wheeled to confront him. "A developer will tear this place down."

"No. The one I talked to said he would remodel it and turn it into a bed and breakfast."

"And you believe him?" She shook her head and sighed as if he was the most gullible man in town.

"Why shouldn't I?"

"Because he's telling you things he thinks you want to hear so he can get a better price." Paige picked up a crystal figurine of a ballerina and studied it before setting it back on a corner table.

Garrett raised his hands out to his sides. "Look at the place. It needs a lot of work."

"What's wrong, Taylor, don't know how to pound a hammer? Or are your hands only used for medicine?"

"I've hammered a nail or two." He folded his arms over his chest. Why was he defending himself to her? "Why should I put a lot of work into the place when I'm going to sell it to a developer?"

Paige bit her lower lip and shook her head, her mood be-coming retrospective and serious. "Because you have pride in this house. It's a reflection of your grandfather. It *is* your grandfather. Every piece of furniture, every picture, every-thing in here belonged to him. He gave it to you because he loved you, and because he trusted you to take care of his legacy."

"Stop the sermon. The only reason you want me to keep this place is because of the museum and your grand-mother."

"That's not true." She stepped over to the fireplace man-tel and picked up a silver framed-photograph, wiping the dust off with the sleeve of her jacket. A gentle smile spread on her lips.

Damn, her full lips were enticing. Kissable. Very kissa-ble.

"This is what you're selling." She strode over to him, smacked the picture into his chest so he had to take it, and then left the room, wandering into the study located across the foyer from the parlor.

Garrett stared at his grandparents and himself in the pho-tograph, their faces smiling back at him. He remembered the picture being taken, but it had been so long ago, in a different time, in a different place in his life. Funny, as a kid he wouldn't have ever imagined selling this place.

Had too much time passed for him to still hold senti-mental attachments to the house, or had he changed, be-come more hardened—or maybe just more practical?

Granny McCormick stepped over the threshold, then halted, seeing Garrett. "Where's Paige?" Granny de-manded.

Garrett hadn't seen the old woman in years, but she looked just the same, with piercing blue-gray eyes and slightly sunken cheeks.

"I'm right here, Granny." Paige hurried over to her. "Did the sheriff tell you the urn was stolen?"

Granny folded her arms, her small red purse dangling

from her forearm. "He stopped me outside. What are you doing in here?"

"Garrett was checking to see if anything was damaged or stolen," Paige said. "You remember Garrett Taylor, don't you Granny?"

Granny glowered at Garrett as if he were a three-eyed monster. A sneer curled her withered upper lip. "I remember him," she grumbled. "But I remember a lad who used to be much kinder and caring of folks in this town, like his granddaddy had been."

Garrett met her eyes before he looked away. He didn't have to explain himself to her. She wasn't the one who would have to plow thousands of dollars into this house to get it livable again. And that's what he would have to do if he decided to keep this dilapidated structure. What would he need with a house this size? Selling it was the smartest financial move he could make, especially at the lucrative price the developer mentioned. The museum could relocate, as could Moonshine McCormick, a.k.a., Granny.

Tonic. Yeah right!

"You might think you've got us licked, young man," Granny said. "But you haven't won yet. Your granddaddy, God rest his soul, had an agreement with the museum that we could remain in this mansion indefinitely."

Garrett narrowed his stare at her. "What agreement?"

Granny smiled smugly. The woman couldn't be more than five feet tall, but she was as tough as any man head and shoulders above her. Despite her age—and she must be well into her eighties by now—she stood erect with her shoulders back. She kept her white hair in a tight bun at the nape of her neck, the same style she had worn for the last thirty years, or at least as far back as Garrett could remember. He couldn't decide whether she was more ornery or stubborn.

"Like I told you, your granddaddy left us a lease," Granny said in her high-pitched, gravelly voice.

"Do you have proof of this?" Garrett glanced at Paige, who seemed as surprised by the news as he was.

"I sure do," Granny said. "I just gotta find it."

"Then by all means look for it." Garrett gestured to the door, and followed Paige and Granny behind the house to the apartment Granny lived in. He remained at the doorstep while the women entered the small studio room. If he recalled correctly, this was one of the hired help's rooms. Was it the cook's? Or the gardener's? He couldn't remember.

Garrett peered around the studio apartment. Granny must have moved her own furniture in; the tables and chairs were made of crude construction and cheap wood. A hot plate, small refrigerator, cupboard, table and five chairs made up her kitchen. A full-sized bed, cot, rocking chair, dresser, night stand, and old television filled the rest of the space.

Garrett had heard Granny kept her still to make moonshine up in the woods, supposedly not far from the mansion. He hadn't seen it, but didn't doubt for a minute that that was where she brewed her "tonic."

Granny put on her thick bifocals, then shuffled through a drawer with papers in it. "I know it's in here somewhere." Wheeling toward Garrett, she shook her gnarled finger at him. "But even if I don't find it, that won't matter. Because an agreement is an agreement. And a person's word is as good as a signed document any day. That's the way it's always been in Patterson." She resumed her search.

*   *   *

"Maybe it's in here," Paige said, opening a bottom drawer.

Garrett shifted his gaze to her. He admired her long legs and rounded hips. When she pulled her long hair to one side, he noticed how it shimmered, even in the dim light of the room. No doubt about it, Paige McCormick had turned into a real beauty.

"Find it?" Granny asked.

"No," Paige said, shutting the drawer. Her face was slightly flushed.

"Well, I can't find it right now," Granny said sternly. "It's probably in my safe deposit box. I can't get it until tomorrow."

Garrett's attention snapped back to the old woman. "Unless you find it, I'm going to continue with my plans." Why shouldn't he? For all he knew Granny had made up the whole story.

"I should have known you wouldn't honor your granddaddy's agreement. Just like you're not keeping the home he wants you to keep. No wonder he's haunting this house."

What was she rambling on about? Did he really care?

"Because you were a friend of my grandfather's, I'll look through his papers. If I find anything at all concerning your agreement, I promise you, I'll honor it."

Garrett met Paige's gaze, nodded, then shut the door behind him. He returned to the front of the mansion and trekked back inside. Was that respect he saw when she looked at him? The thought irritated him. Why should he care what she thought? Garrett suddenly realized that Paige McCormick was getting under his skin, and way too fast. Maybe he should heed his father's advice and stay away from those McCormicks.

His father always said they were nothing but trouble.

*   *   *

Paige watched Garrett disappear behind the closed door. Each time he came near, she felt a spark between them. He could be dangerous to her, much more dangerous than the problem of Granny and the museum.

Paige directed her attention to her grandmother. "Where else could you have put it?"

Granny dropped into a wooden chair at the table, and sighed. "Get me something sweet, dear. I eat when I'm frustrated."

"You'd never know it, Granny. You're as thin as can be. If you get any skinnier you'll disappear." Paige opened the cupboard, pushed aside cans of soup, finding a package of cookies in the back. After giving Granny three, she decided to put the rest in the cookie jar. As a little girl, Paige remembered this honey bear cookie jar was always filled when she visited. A warmth rose in her heart at the fond memory. She rubbed her finger over the chipped rim before she removed the lid.

Something inside caught her eye.

Reaching in, she lifted out a folded piece of paper covered in crumbs. "Granny, what's this?" Paige asked, opening it.

"That's it!" Granny said, smacking the table top with the palm of her hand. "I remember now, I put it in there for safekeeping. I figured I'd never lose it since my weakness was cookies." Granny jabbed her finger in the air in Paige's direction. "See, it's official. That Taylor boy can't toss me out."

Paige read the notarized document, then groaned. "Granny, this agreement states it's only valid if the museum turns a profit." She met Granny's stare. "The museum hasn't turned a profit in, well, has it ever?"

Granny hesitated. "Maybe not, but that doesn't mean the Taylor boy has to know that."

"How have you been keeping the museum going?"

Reluctantly, she admitted, "My tonic money."

The realization of how much this museum meant to Granny suddenly hit Paige. Her grandmother had kept this town's history alive with her own money, money she could have used for retirement. Whether Granny would admit it or not, the pride she felt for the McCormick ancestors was as inherent in Granny as it was in Paige. Credibility wasn't a common characteristic for the McCormick clan, but the urn helped give them that, as little as it was.

Paige would take anything she could get, anything she could cling to. Apparently, Granny would, too.

"I'll see if I can catch up with Garrett," Paige said, then paused at the door. "Granny, what are we going to do about the urn?"

Worry lines appeared at the corners of Granny's eyes. "I'll call the insurance company tomorrow."

"Well, I guess if there's a bright side to this situation, it would be that Grandpa's ashes weren't still in the urn."

Granny eyes widened, then she quickly looked away.

"You did scatter Grandpa's ashes by the lake like he wanted, didn't you?"

"I meant to," she said defensively. "I just never got around to it."

"So Grandpa's been kidnapped?" Paige fell speechless.

"Having him in the urn made me feel as if he was still around." Granny crossed her arms over her chest.

With conviction, Paige said, "Somehow, I'll find the thief, and we'll get our urn—and Grandpa back!" She strode to the door and rested her hand on the doorknob.

Over her shoulder, she added, "But first, I'll see if Garrett Taylor will honor his grandfather's agreement."

"Don't bet on it," Granny mumbled.

Paige hustled out the door and raced around to the front. Noticing Garrett's truck still parked out front, she jumped the steps two at a time, barging through the front door without knocking. "Garrett," she called. "Are you here?"

She heard a rustling above. Breezing through the foyer, she ascended the long, curved staircase. When she reached the second floor, she called his name again.

The forest green walls created a dark hallway. Paige didn't see lights on in any of the rooms on either side of the stairs. She shivered.

Something boomed overhead, making her glance towards the ceiling. He must be on the third floor. Paige's heart beat a little faster. Granny and her friends had told her they had heard strange sounds coming from the third floor of the mansion. Wouldn't it be just like the folks in this town to stick around even *after* they had died?

Summing up her courage, she climbed the stairs, the old floorboards creaking with each step she took. She paused on the landing and glanced around. Most of the third floor was taken up by the music room, and short hallways were on either side of it. The walls were bright and cheery, painted in pastel yellow with white trim, quite the opposite from the forest green walls of the second floor.

The French ornately carved double doors to the music room were closed, and Paige wasn't sure whether to barge in or not. "Garrett?" she called.

"In here," he hollered from within the room. A loud grunt followed as if he was moving something heavy.

Paige advanced through the doors, then halted, staring in

awe at the domed glass ceiling. "Wow," she whispered. "This room's amazing."

The sheets had been removed from the furniture, and most of the sofa and chairs—padded in an elegant maroon and gold velvet—were placed against the wall. Large windows fronted the room, which looked out over the grounds, and to the rolling hills in the distance. In the corner was a shiny black grand piano; pushed up against another wall was an upright piano.

Pride rang in Garrett's voice as he said, "My grandfather called it the music room. My grandparents had all their parties in here."

Paige let her gaze drift from the classical paintings decorating the walls to Garrett. She flushed red. He had stripped down to a gray T-shirt, jeans and shoes. His clothes fit him snugly, emphasizing his well-toned athletic physique. She didn't like the reaction she was having by merely looking at Garrett, but he was a sight to see. His biceps bulged and stretched the material of his sleeves. A curl of hair fell over his forehead, the strands the same black as his thick eyebrows.

She met his stare. He had to be the most handsome man she had ever seen.

"What are you doing?" she asked.

"I'm trying to get the place straightened up a little before the developer comes."

"You're going to have to tell him the deal's off."

Undoubtedly, his suspicions drew his brows together. "Why's that?"

She waved the paper in the air, then advanced over to him. "We found the lease agreement."

Garrett's grin faded as he snatched the paper from her

hand. He took his time reading the small print. "This agreement is null and void."

Paige crossed her arms over her chest. "You can't do that."

"I didn't. Your grandmother did."

She tilted her head. "What are you talking about?"

"The museum has to turn a profit in order for this agreement to be valid. We both know it's not profitable." A cocky, smug smile appeared on his perfectly shaped mouth. His shoulders relaxed.

He had put her on the defense, and she would fight back to the bitter end for Granny, if she had to. She didn't know what else to do.

"You're wrong. Check my grandmother's books." She hoped Granny had doctored the books, and could pretty well guess that Granny had covered her bases by doing so.

Garrett chuckled. "I don't care much for reading fiction. Or am I wrong?" He lifted his brows.

Paige gritted her teeth, squeezing her lips together. Darn him.

"I didn't think so." Garrett tossed the paper on the piano, turned his attention to the gold and red settee, and moved it against the wall.

Paige's mind raced for an argument. Garrett couldn't win that easily. She wouldn't let him. "I don't think a judge would see it your way. And even if he or she did, it would take months before it went to court."

Garrett straightened, shoulders back. He looked anything but happy.

Good. She had struck a nerve.

"I should have guessed a McCormick wouldn't keep her word."

His comment cut swift and without warning, straight to

her heart. Her tone turned glacial. "I'd say it's a Taylor who's not keeping his word."

Garrett picked up a rag lying on the piano, then threw it back down in obvious frustration. "We both know the figures your grandmother has in those books are bogus."

Paige didn't flinch, holding a firm, steady gaze with him. "I don't know that. And you don't either." She tilted her head. "Of course, I suppose we could hire an accountant to come in and audit the books." She glanced to the ceiling and tapped her index finger on her chin. "Hmmm, that might take weeks." Meeting his angry glare, she added, "Maybe even months. Either way, looks like that developer of yours is going to have to wait."

"No way!" Garrett paced behind the piano, running his fingers through his hair.

Enjoying the position she was in, Paige waited for his response. She had just put a Taylor at a disadvantage, something that hadn't been done often in Patterson.

After a long moment of silence, Garrett said, "I'll give her one month, but I have conditions that dear old Granny will have to meet. First, I'll hire an impartial and honest accountant to keep track of the museum books. Second, if she can't show a profit in one month, then the lease is voided, and Granny and the museum will have to look for a new home—" he held up his index finger, "without a fight."

She suppressed a sigh of relief. Thank God! She had bought Granny some time. "What about the developer?" She was no dummy. Garrett wouldn't give up that easily.

He shrugged. "I fully intend to strike a deal, but it could take weeks to negotiate and close." He raised his arms and motioned around the room. "I'll need that time to clean the place up."

"What happens if the museum does turn a profit? What then?"

"I'll put a revision in the contract. Either the museum will stay or I'll provide a building for it."

Paige strode over to him, her hand extended. She tried but couldn't hide her wide smile. "It's a deal."

Garrett and she shook hands.

She could feel the strength in his grip.

"Could you please put this agreement in writing?" Paige asked, as sweetly as possible.

Suddenly, his grip tightened.

Paige tried not to flinch or yelp in pain. Instead she met his challenge by squeezing his hand harder.

"What's the matter, Paige? Don't you trust me?" He released his hold.

"I don't know, Garrett," she said, emphasizing his name. "Should I trust a Taylor?"

He laughed, the sound rich, husky, and genuine. "I do believe I've met my match."

Turning, she strode to the door and paused. She glanced back at him. "I'll expect the papers sometime tomorrow."

With a stiff hand, he saluted her.

Paige managed to get down to the second floor before she released a giggle. She could get used to telling a Taylor what to do.

Then the thought that Garrett let her have her way flitted through her mind. Her confidence started to dwindle. She shook her head. No. She had him at a disadvantage.

At this point, she would take anything she could get, and hope it lasted.

Two days later, Garrett had kept his word and had provided the amendment to the lease, and an accountant.

Paige heard a vehicle pull up to the front of the main house. She peered out the museum window and spotted a man—dressed in a black business suit, and carrying a brief-case—getting out of a Lexus with Garrett. The other man had to be the developer. She expelled a frustrated breath. Taylor didn't waste any time, did he?

Paige quickly stuffed postcards into a holder in the museum gift shop, a small area off to one side of the museum, which sold books, book markers, pencils, pens, and hand-made crafts. "Granny, can you hold the fort down for a few minutes? I want to go check on something."

Granny didn't question her, but instead nodded, absorbed in a book she was reading.

By the time Paige exited the museum, the two men had entered the mansion. What could she do to stop this sale? Perhaps persuade the developer that this mansion would be a bad investment. Garrett would surely hate her for it, but why should she care?

Paige entered through the front door, pausing to listen. Hearing murmuring in a room beyond the library and par-lor, she ambled closer, hoping a brilliant idea might come to her at any second.

She ran her finger along the wall. Even the layers of dust couldn't hide the beautiful, rich, carved wainscoting, the intricately designed molding on the ceiling, and the hard-wood floors that covered the foyer and first-level hallways. Sconces, electrically wired, dotted the walls, casting dra-matic lighting in the halls and rooms.

How could Garrett sell this place? Every room, every nook and cranny was so beautiful, each room having its own distinct style, and all of them elegant.

The double doors to the dining room were open. Paige invited herself in and took a moment to view the exquisite furnishings. A long, cherry table took center stage, and looked large enough to seat at least twelve people. There was a matching sideboard and ornately-carved case, a marbled fireplace, and a large painting of Rocky and his wife, Gretta, hanging above the mantel.

Completing her journey of the room, Paige swung her attention to Garrett.

"May I help you?" he said in a very formal manner, almost as if he had never met her before.

"I thought I might be able to help," Paige said, then hurried on before Garrett could tell her to get the heck out. "Did you mention about the cracks in the fireplace in the parlor? I noticed them the other day when I was in here."

Because she knew what Garrett's reaction would be, Paige avoided looking at him, and instead focused on the developer. She guessed he was in his early fifties, a nice-looking man, neatly groomed with dark hair, and graying at his temples.

Paige strode over to him as though she owned the place and extended her hand. "I'm Paige McCormick. My grandmother runs the museum out of the conservatory."

"Lester Bradford." He frowned.

Just as she had suspected. Garrett hadn't mentioned the museum yet. Which she would use to her advantage. "Did Garrett tell you about the lease agreement the museum and my grandmother have with the Taylors?" She knew he hadn't. That's what made this situation so delightful.

Lester turned toward Garrett. "No, he hasn't."

"I was just getting to that," Garrett said, stepping closer. "Don't worry about it, Les. By the time we close this deal, the museum will be gone."

"Not if we turn a profit," Paige reminded him, then gave Lester a sweet, winning smile. "You see, Lester, before

Rocky Taylor died, he was kind enough to lease the conservatory to the museum. The museum is a big tourist draw, especially during the summer. The museum is to remain at the mansion indefinitely." Okay, so she exaggerated a tad. What did it matter?

Lester smiled, looking much too pleased by the news. "That sounds good for business." He stepped by her and wandered out of the room.

Paige's smile faded. She briefly closed her eyes. How stupid could she be? She thought the idea of people pouring in and out of the museum would discourage the developer, not encourage him. Of course, he would want a lot of people around, especially tourists, so they would stay at the mansion.

Garrett stepped up behind her and placed his hand on her shoulder. He leaned towards her and whispered in her ear, "Thanks, Paige. Who knows, by the end of the meeting you just might sell the place for me." As he walked away, he gave a deep-throated chuckle.

Paige chewed on her lower lip. No, she couldn't give up. She had to find a way to discourage the developer. Turning towards the door, she chased after them. "You know, Lester, the mansion's been sitting idle for almost two years. As you can tell, there's been no upkeep at all during that time. It might be a good idea to check for dry rot. And let's not forget the plumbing and electrical work. I bet those need updating."

Garrett led the way up the stairs with Paige following on their heels. When they reached the landing, Lester abruptly halted, turned to Paige and said, "Young lady, I've been in this line of work for thirty years. I'm well aware of what goes into remodeling an old house such as this one."

While the developer reprimanded her, she glanced over Lester's shoulder, and noticed Garrett's wide smile and raised brows.

"There isn't anything you could tell me that I haven't already checked, or already noticed," Lester said.

The front door downstairs slammed, followed by someone traipsing in the house and up the stairs. They waited for the person to appear. Paige heard Garrett mutter, "Oh great," when Granny joined them.

"I'm sure this boy hasn't told you the biggest surprise in this place," Granny said.

"Why don't we look at the master bedroom?" Garrett interjected.

Lester raised his hand to halt Garrett, and waited for Granny to continue.

Paige quickly jumped in saying, "This is my grandmother, Isabel McCormick. She is the caretaker of the museum. Granny, this is Lester Bradford, the developer who might buy the mansion."

"He know about our lease?" Granny asked in a challenging tone.

"Yes, I'm aware of it and everything else about the mansion," Lester said.

"Well, that's where you're wrong." Granny said. "Because I'd bet my last dollar that the Taylor boy has avoided telling you about the biggest secret of this big, old house."

"And what's that?" Lester asked.

"It's haunted!"

Chapter Three

Garrett couldn't believe his ears. The woman was not only desperate, but she had become addle-brained. "Les, don't listen to her. She wants the museum to remain where it is, and she's afraid if I sell it to you, then she'll be evicted along with the museum."

"That's not true!" Granny said. "This house *is* haunted. Ask anyone. I'm not the only one who's heard the piano playing at night, and the sounds of footsteps walking all over the mansion. Others have even seen the ghost of Rocky Taylor appear in the windows."

"Oh, please," Garrett said. "This is ridiculous. There's no such thing as ghosts." He motioned for Lester to follow him down the hall into the master bedroom.

The walls, painted in pastel green, brought a sense of spring to the room. A large, teak wardrobe with ornate floral carvings took up nearly one wall. The bed's head and foot boards matched the intricate carvings on the wardrobe;

and at each corner were massive, round bedposts. Its gold bedspread matched the velvet chairs, and a large rug, patterned in red, yellow, and black, covered most of the hard wood floor.

Paintings of women in large, wide-brimmed hats and long, white, flowing dresses adorned the walls, giving the room a Victorian ambience. The vanity table was still cluttered with bottles of perfume, a silver hairbrush and comb, and a jewelry box.

Garrett tried to suppress the memories that tugged at his heart each time he came into this room, and spotted his grandmother's musical jewelry box. Was his grandmother's ring still inside, the ring she had told him to give to his bride someday? Well, that day still hadn't happened. And it was mostly his fault. He'd had opportunities, but the relationships never worked out. Chemistry had been missing, that instant spark that attracted a man to a woman, that intangible key ingredient he had never felt before, but somehow knew existed.

"You could turn this into two rooms," Garrett said, hoping that by changing the subject he could rid himself of any sentimentality and guilt. He had to sell this place to protect his mother, and keep her past—their past—a secret.

Out of sight, out of mind. Right?

Lester replied with a sharp nod.

Paige remained at the door while Granny trailed behind them, like a shadow. The cantankerous old woman didn't intend to give up. Garrett figured as much. She was like a bad penny, always showing up.

His glance strayed to Paige and remained on her, following the gentle curves of her lips, cheeks, eyes, and brows. Pure femininity. That's how he would describe her, yet she had an undeniable strength that most men would envy. He liked how she challenged him, even when the odds were stacked against her.

Yes. She definitely stirred something in him that sent aches rushing through his body.

"Rocky's spirit started making noises the very same night this young Taylor boy came to town. Now, if that doesn't answer a lot of questions, I don't know what does," Granny said.

Garrett snorted out a breath. He was sure this was another McCormick scheme—except for one thing—Paige wasn't joining in.

He did *not* believe in ghosts. Even if this wasn't an attempt by Moonshine McCormick to dissuade Lester from buying the mansion, the sounds could be explained away. She was an old lady. Her mind was playing tricks on her. Old houses always creak and groan.

After surveying the walls and bathroom, Lester returned to the bedroom. "Have you seen a ghost in this house?" Lester asked. He sounded skeptical.

"Well, actually Booker Vee saw the ghost looking out the window from this very room. But I've heard plenty, like footsteps walking in the house, doors slamming shut, and the piano playing like there's no tomorrow. Other people in town have heard it too. In fact, just the other day my friend, Lily Fern said she saw a glowing figure floating through one of the rooms," Granny said.

"Lily also claims she can communicate with plants and animals," Garrett quickly added.

Granny folded her arms across her chest. "Then what about Jean Welsh? She saw lights flickering in the parlor just last night."

"The wires are loose." Garrett thrust his hands in his jeans pockets. This woman was irritating him. He glared at

Paige. "And what about you? I suppose you've seen or heard something too?"

"No, I haven't. But I haven't been in town long."

"This is just another scam," Garrett said. "It's not going to work."

"I don't think it's a scam, Garrett." Paige sounded sincere and serious.

After releasing a frustrated sigh, he said, "Les, why don't we look at the rest of the bedrooms, then the music room?"

Granny gasped. "The music room is where the ghost of Rocky Taylor plays the piano at night."

"Ladies," Garrett said, with as much restraint as possible. "I'm trying to conduct business here. I'd appreciate it if you would show yourselves out."

Garrett stepped by Paige. He caught a whiff of her perfume, triggering a warmth to race through his veins. Great. He didn't need this on top of Granny's fictitious ghost stories. Selling the mansion should be his only focus, his top priority. Once business was completed, he could resume his life and practice in Portland. And he'd no longer have to worry about his mother's past catching up with her.

Lester squinted and stared out into space, deep in thought. "You know, if I advertised this place as haunted, it might bring in tourists. Could be good for business. That's an excellent marketing strategy." Lester's enthusiasm increased.

From behind, Garrett leaned into Paige. "You and your grandmother may sell this place for me yet. I may have to give you two a commission." His breath stirred the strands of her hair.

Paige looked over her shoulder, giving him a frigid glance. "Come on, Granny. We've got a museum to run."

Garrett watched Paige until she disappeared from sight.

So many emotions churned inside him. She did that to him. That, and a lot more. There was something about Paige McCormick that got his blood boiling. Sure, she had the curves, and a beautiful face, but there was something more to it. Something he couldn't quite put his finger on. An attraction not easily defined, and foreign to him.

Lester cleared his throat, jolting Garrett back to reality. Slightly embarrassed, Garrett quickly returned to the subject. "Let me show you the bedroom across the hall."

Turning his back to Lester, he led the way into the next room.

Later in the day, after a quick dinner, Garrett began to clean his grandfather's study. It took a lot of elbow work because the dust was so thick on everything in the room. Books filled the shelves—old leather-bounds, some modern hardcovers—and the subjects ranged from classic fiction to gardening. Two large windows, accented with ivy patterned curtains, allowed ample light in the room for reading.

Along with a large mahogany desk and leather chair, the room accommodated two dark sofas, a recliner, and several wooden chairs. His grandfather had come in here often and would read for hours about anything and everything. He had been one of the most knowledgeable men Garrett had ever known, and his mind had remained sharp until the day he'd died.

Was he doing the right thing in selling the mansion? Did he have a choice?

Lester's unexpected visit hadn't given Garrett time to fix the place up and get it ready to show. At least Lester promised to return in a month and look it over again, then make his decision. By then, Garrett hoped to have Granny and the museum out of his hair.

The front door creaked open, drawing Garrett out of his thoughts.

"Hello, anybody here?"

Garrett recognized Paige's voice and his mood suddenly brightened.

"In here." When she stepped into the room, he noticed his heart beat quicker. Annoyed by his reaction to her, he said gruffly, "What do you want?"

She frowned. "I'm looking for Buster. Have you seen him?"

Jealousy flickered through Garrett, the feeling so new, so raw. "Who's Buster?"

"My cat."

Relieved, he relaxed. "No. Sorry I haven't. Did you look outside?"

"Yes, and I called him, but he doesn't come. It's not like Buster to miss a meal. I thought he might have come in here earlier with Granny. Would you mind if I looked around?"

Garrett shrugged. "Not at all. I'll help you look." He followed Paige as she walked toward the kitchen, watching and liking the sway of her hips.

"Here kitty, kitty, kitty. Buster, where are you?" Paige asked.

Garrett heard the strain in her voice. No doubt, she loved Buster a great deal. As a veterinarian, he saw many people who became very attached to their animals, and who took wonderful care of them. He was pleased that Paige was one of those people.

They heard a crash upstairs.

Garrett met Paige's eyes before she hastened up to the

second floor, jumping two steps at a time. He trailed on her heels. Glancing in each room, she rushed down the hall, darting into the last one.

"Buster," she said sternly. "What have you done?" She glanced over her shoulder at Garrett. "I'll pay for the damaged figurine." Paige walked over to the cat, but he bolted under the bed. "Buster, what's wrong with you?"

"Maybe I can help," Garrett said. "I'll take this side. You take the other." He knelt, then looked under the bed. Just as he thought, the cat had a dead mouse and didn't intend on sharing it with anyone. "Here, kitty. Come on." Garrett used a gentle voice, but it didn't matter. The cat's backside was literally to the wall, and he didn't intend to budge, at least not until he finished his meal.

"I have an idea." Paige returned from the hall with a broom. Kneeling on the opposite side of the bed from Garrett, she poked Buster gently with the handle. Quick as greased lightening, the cat picked up the mouse and streaked toward Garrett.

Before he could grab the cat, Buster scampered by Garrett and onto the bed. Garrett hustled to his feet and reached for the animal. Paige did the same. They lunged for the cat at the same time, their heads colliding. Buster scampered out the door. For a moment they both stood there, stunned.

"Are you all right?" Garrett asked, his head throbbing.

Paige slowly sat down on the bed and laughed, while she rubbed her forehead. "You have a hard head."

"Yours wasn't exactly soft." Garrett came around the bed and sat down beside her. "Here, let me take a look at that. I am a doctor, remember?"

"Of animals," she said.

"Humans are animals."

"Some more than others." Paige laughed again, and

didn't protest when he examined the red mark near her hairline.

He ran his fingers over her soft, smooth skin, then down the side of her face, stopping at her chin. He gazed into her eyes. "I think you're going to be just fine." His voice came out low and husky. "Would you like me to kiss it for you?"

Even though he tried to play off the moment in a joking fashion, his tone and actions said otherwise. He leaned into her, touching his mouth to hers. Her lips were warm, soft, and giving. Garrett didn't need any more encouragement. He slid his hand to the nape of her neck, then deepened the kiss.

Paige McCormick did something to him. He couldn't recall another woman who could ignite a fire in him like she could. Was it because she had always been off-limits to him?

No. There was something more to it than that.

Paige's hands slowly rose to his chest, and she lifted her head. "This isn't a good idea."

"Why? Didn't you like it?"

"Your kiss was very nice, but we're on opposite sides of an important issue right now."

Garrett released a sigh and fixed his stare on a painting on the wall. "I guess you're right." For a moment, silence lingered between them, but it wasn't an uncomfortable silence, it was one more of disappointment.

Without warning, loud, sullen classical music roared from the upstairs, causing both of them to jump.

Paige gasped. "Who's playing the piano?"

"I don't know."

"Unless . . ."

"Unless what?" Garrett asked.

"Granny said this house was haunted. Remember, she had said she'd heard a ghost playing the piano," Paige said.

Garrett frowned. "There's no such thing as ghosts."

"Then who's playing the piano?"

"Let's go find out." Before she could refuse, he took her by the hand and led the way up to the third floor. The doors to the music room were closed. The loud music caused the walls and floor to vibrate.

"I'm sure I left these doors open," Garrett mumbled.

As quickly as it started, the music stopped.

Paige yanked her hand free. "I don't want to go in."

Garrett twisted the handle, shoved the door wide, and charged into the room.

The moon glistened through the windows, casting an eerie glow to the room. Garrett grappled for the light switch and found it. The room now looked just like—a very large room.

"See. No ghosts." He walked into the center of the room.

"What about the piano playing by itself?" Paige asked, staying near the door. She looked ready to bolt at any second.

He crooked his finger. "Follow me."

"I think I'm fine right here."

"There's a player piano against the wall over there." He pointed at the far end of the room. "It probably malfunctioned." That sounded reasonable, logical.

"Nevertheless, I—I think I'll be going now. I don't intend to wait around for Rocky to return," Paige said.

"Wait—"

Paige hurried away before he could talk some sense into her.

Garrett listened to her move down the stairs, through the

house. When the front door slammed shut, disappointment overcame him. Damn. He didn't want her to leave.

One thing he felt certain about, though, was that Paige wasn't involved with this scheme. Her fear was genuine. But Garrett knew this was nothing but a hoax.

Once outside, Paige paused on the front porch to get a better look at the button she had found near the door of the music room. She examined the white pearl-shaped button. No doubt about it, Granny's favorite sweater had these very same buttons on it.

She returned to the apartment to find Granny there with her poker buddies, smoking cigars and drinking moonshine. Granny wore her black-framed glasses, along with her green dealer's hat. She shuffled the deck like a pro. Her bony hands worked quickly as she dealt the cards.

The usual gang was there: Zoe Bockner, Lily Fern, Jean Welsh, Booker Vee, and Vivian Perish. They met once a week, and jokingly called it the "Bridge Club."

Paige watched as everyone tossed a quarter in the center of the table. "Granny, did you hear the piano playing just a few minutes ago?"

Everyone at the table exchanged glances. "Sure did," Granny said, while keeping her eyes on her cards.

Lily said, "I feel the ghost of Rocky with us now."

Paige looked around the room, but sensed nothing, felt nothing, not even a cold draft.

"Before Rocky's death he used to play with us, you know," Booker said, exhaling a puff of cigar smoke. "He'd always tease me, saying he was going to butcher my pet pig, and have him for dinner." Booker smiled.

Paige could still hear the Southern drawl in Booker's voice. Paige had known him her entire life, and she loved him dearly. He was one of the very few in town who had always treated her and her family well, even after her father's reputation had smeared the McCormick name. She appreciated having Booker as a friend. On more than one occasion, his ample height and large frame came in handy.

"Rocky Taylor played poker with you guys?" Paige asked in surprise.

"He sure did," Booker said. "We loved it when Rocky joined the table. He was one of the worst poker players you'd ever seen. So we all made lots of money off of him." Nods around the table followed. "He was welcome at our table any time." Booker let out a rich, deep chuckle.

"I don't feel his presence," Paige said.

"That's because you don't have the gift," Zoe said. "Like Lily does."

"Does anyone else feel his presence?" Paige didn't mean to sound challenging, but that's how it came out.

"Sometimes I think I do," Booker said. "Like now. I can almost smell his expensive cigar smoke. He always was a generous man. Shared everything, his cigars, his fine brandy."

"Hey, watch your tongue," Granny said. "My moonshine's the best liquor in all of Oregon."

"Right you are. My apologies." Booker winked at Paige.

Paige wanted to stay on the subject of the haunted house, but she didn't want to be too pushy about it, because Granny and her friends would undoubtedly clam up if she pressed them. So Paige watched the hand play out, thinking rapidly.

Booker let out a whooping victory laugh as he used both hands to gather the winning pot. "You're good luck to me, Paige. You'd better stay for awhile. Last time we played, I lost big. I need to recoup my empty pocket."

While Granny shuffled the deck again, Paige returned to the subject. "Garrett said there's no such thing as ghosts."

"What does that boy know?" Granny said.

An uncomfortable tension took hold in the room. No doubt Garrett Taylor was a dirty word at this table. "I was in the house looking for Buster when the piano started to play."

"You were?" Granny sounded uninterested, as if she wasn't even listening. "How many cards do you want Jean?"

"Three. 'Who steals my purse steals trash', " Jean said.

"Shakespeare's *Othello*," Vivian said.

Jean smiled. "Correct."

Again, Paige tried to steer the conversation back to the hauntings in the mansion. "When I was in the music room, I found a white pearl-shaped button. Don't you have ones just like this on your favorite sweater?"

From the corner of her eye, Granny glimpsed over, then returned her attention to the game. "Can't say I do. Can't say I don't."

"Sure you do, Granny. On your white sweater. Were you in the music room today?"

"Nope. I avoid that house as much as possible. Especially with Rocky on his rampage."

"Rampage?"

"Yeah. He's really steamed up about his grandson trying to sell the place," Granny said.

Everyone nodded as if that was common knowledge.

"Then how'd your button get up there?" Paige said.

"I told you that's not mine." Granny sounded defensive and a bit angry, maybe even hurt. "If you're so sure it's mine, why don't you look in my closet."

Paige went to the closet and opened the door. She immediately found Granny's sweater. Sure enough, the button matched the ones on the sweater—but Granny's sweater wasn't missing any buttons. Paige looked closely at the threads sewn around each button.

"Well?" Granny asked.

"It's not yours. Your sweater isn't missing any buttons."

"Told you so." Granny sounded smug, and confident. Too confident.

"Do you think Rocky has met Gloria Swanson on the other side?" Vivian asked. Vivian loved old movies. Her home was filled with old movie posters and pictures. Often when Paige had walked by Vivian's home, Paige had seen Vivian dressed up in costume and acting out a scene.

Paige returned to the table to watch and listen.

"Forget Gloria Swanson, Rocky should meet Marilyn Monroe," Booker said, raising his brows and grinning ear to ear.

"Who would you want to see, Granny?" Paige asked.

She hesitated a moment before she said, "Your Grandpa. I surely do miss him."

The comment brought a lump to Paige's throat. Granny and Grandpa McCormick had been inseparable for fifty-six years. They were each other's best friend, through thick and thin. Paige had always envied their relationship. Someday, she hoped to find that close relationship with a man. Someday.

Garrett came to Paige's mind. He was definitely handsome, and muscularly built—and his voice. . . . There was something very soothing about his voice, a calm, gentleness that put a person at ease. And his hands, his touch, had been tender, caring: it had warmed her insides. Just thinking about it made her long for him again.

"Your face is a bit flushed, dear," Zoe said to Paige. "Are you feeling all right?"

Heat rushed to her cheeks. She was sure she looked like a cherry tomato. "I am a bit warm. I think I'll take a walk outside." Wanting to run outside, she used as much restraint as she could muster and sauntered to the door, pausing to snatch her coat off the rack. Before she shut the door, she peered back at the table. The group was grinning and exchanging glances.

Did they know what she was thinking and feeling? She couldn't be that transparent. Sure she was attracted to Garrett, but her feelings didn't go beyond that. She was no fool. Garrett Taylor had always been, and would always be, out of her league. The richest kid in town always married the prom queen, not the girl with a chip on her shoulder—and who had an ex-con for a father.

Yet he hadn't married the prom queen. Not only that, he'd left town right after high school, only to return now. Why?

She ran her finger over her lips. She could still feel his mouth on hers, and a stirring deep inside, a feeling she had never experienced before. One touch from Garrett and her knees went weak. Did he have to be such a good kisser?

Paige shook her head. She had to stop this crazy thinking. Absently, she strolled the Taylor grounds. She wasn't sure how long she had been walking before she ended up at the Taylor family cemetery plot that resided between the mansion and the woods.

The wind picked up, whistling through the trees. Thunder rumbled and lightening flashed in the far distance. Black clouds were heading directly for Patterson. Thankfully, the rain hadn't come yet.

She closed her eyes, and let the cool breeze caress her face.

"Do you often take walks through cemeteries on stormy nights?" Garrett asked.

Paige gasped and whirled around. She could see only his silhouette in the shadows. "It's not nice to sneak up on people."

"Who said I was nice?" Garrett stepped from the darkness into the moonlight. He wore a grin, but his eyes held something else. Maybe he had been thinking about their kiss, too.

Paige felt her heart leap. Over the years, she had taught herself to let her head do the thinking, not her heart. That's exactly what she wanted to do now. So why couldn't she?

Garrett was dangerous. The last thing she needed was to let him worm his way into her heart. Didn't she have enough to worry about? He was the one behind all her worries! She should be thinking of him as the enemy, and nothing more.

"Well, you have a point," she said with ease. "If I recall, only your grandparents were nice."

He tilted his head slightly back as if her words had struck him in the face.

Good. That's what she wanted. Something to keep him at arm's length.

"Well, you have to admit, you McCormicks have a few vices of your own." He nodded in the direction of Granny's apartment, keeping his hands in his coat pockets. Puffs of warm air appeared when he spoke. "I'll bet your grandmother is in there right now with her friends playing poker and drinking 'tonic'."

"From what I understand, your grandfather often joined them," Paige said.

Garrett smiled. "Yes, he did." He stepped closer, then paused, resting his hand on a large headstone. "He told me he would lose on purpose. He said it was a way of helping folks out without them knowing about it."

Paige's heart warmed. "Rocky was a good man."

"Yeah. I miss him." Garrett's voice turned a bit thick. He cleared his throat. "You never answered me."

Paige frowned.

"Do you often take walks in cemeteries?" He lifted his brows in a mock question. "Don't tell me you're hoping to see a ghost?"

"Quite the opposite. I'm hoping not to see one. Don't you think the ghosts would be bored with Patterson, especially the ones that used to live here before they died?" Paige tried to make light of the spooky topic.

Garrett's tone grew serious. "You know, there's no such thing as ghosts."

"So you've told me."

"This whole ghost story is another McCormick scheme, concocted by your grandmother, and it won't work."

Paige's muscles tensed. "Why do you always assume it's my family that's up to no good? My father made some mistakes. You and this town won't let any of us forget that."

"Is that why most of your family moved away?" Garrett asked.

"Do you blame them?"

"Is that why *you* moved away?" He took a step closer so they were only a few feet apart.

She met his inquiring gaze. "I moved away so I could make something of myself. And I did."

"I know. I found your books in my grandfather's library. You're very good." He sounded sincere.

"Thank you." She had been told by others that her work was good, but she had never gauged her success on what others said. Yet satisfaction swept over her, knowing Garrett approved. Why should his opinion mean so much to her? She shouldn't care.

"So why'd you move away?" Paige asked.

Garrett averted his gaze. "I guess for same reasons you did," he mumbled.

"You guess? You don't know?"

He pinned her with a glare. "What's it matter?"

"You asked me, and I answered you. It's only fair you answer me honestly." Paige folded her arms across her chest.

He drew in a deep breath, and expelled it in a rush. The mist of his breath swirled, then quickly dissipated. "I guess to find my freedom. Make my own decisions."

"I don't blame you. Your father was controlling."

Garrett's eyes widened. Then he quickly masked his surprise.

"I never had that problem," Paige said. "Of course, my father was in and out of jail most of the time. How could he be controlling when he wasn't around?" She tried to laugh, producing a hard, brittle sound. "I had my share of problems, but I wouldn't have traded places with you."

"Why's that?" Garrett asked.

"Your father expected you to be the best at everything. I wouldn't have wanted that kind of pressure, especially at a young age. But you handled it well."

"Did I?"

She had his full attention. "Garrett, you did everything the best. You were the best athlete, the smartest kid in school, the best looking—" Paige wanted to kick herself for letting that one slip.

Garrett reached out for the front of her coat and pulled her to him. "And what about now? Do you find me good looking?"

How could she not? Every angle of his face, his strong jaw, aristocratic nose, and thick eyebrows exuded manliness. But Paige couldn't lie. Unlike her father, she was terrible at it.

"Garrett," she said, her voice steady, but her heart pounding, "you're one of the most handsome men I've ever met. And a good kisser."

"Would you like me to kiss you again?"

No! she shouted to herself. But her conviction quickly melted the instant he drew her close. The word slipped out before she could stop herself. "Yes."

Lowering his head, Garrett captured her mouth with his. This time, his kiss was filled with hunger.

Paige tried to tell herself that the sensation springing up inside was due to the cold evening air, or maybe from the eerie atmosphere in a cemetery. But she knew the truth. The tingle was caused by Garrett, by his touch, and experienced kisses, that left her breathless and trembling. He did that to her. Every time she came near him, she felt a connection, a chemistry.

Paige struggled with her conflicting feelings. She liked the excitement he ignited in her, but at the same time, she didn't want it, or understand it. At the moment, Garrett Taylor was her grandmother's enemy, which made him her enemy.

She fought for sensibility. What was wrong with her? Where had that wall gone, the one she could always erect to push a man away?

Garrett lifted his head, the warmth of his breath caressing

her cheek. When he reclaimed her lips, tendrils of his hair brushed against her skin.

The pressure of his hand and the feel of his lips were all touches she hadn't felt in a long time. Too long.

She quivered.

His arms wound around her tighter as he dropped kisses along her cheek, then nestled his face in her hair. "It's cold out here tonight."

Paige felt anything but cold. A warmth spread through her, to every fingertip and every toe. Her pulse raced for one reason, and one reason only—his touch. The realization almost made her laugh. While traveling the world, she had never met a man who could do that. And where did she find him? In the little town of Patterson, a place she couldn't get far enough away from.

"Why don't we go inside? We could drink wine and lie in front of a warm fire."

"Garrett," Paige said breathlessly. "That's not a good idea. This is not a good idea." Paige took a couple of steps back to distance herself from him. Perhaps that would help her to think more clearly.

"You said that before," Garrett said.

"And I'm saying it again. You and I wouldn't work. I'm only staying long enough to help Granny. My work takes me all over the world. I can't get involved with you, or anybody." She sighed, unsure if that thought brought her relief, or sadness.

Feeling another presence, Paige looked over her shoulder. She sucked in a sharp breath, her stare locked on the woods.

A form glided through the trees, heading in their direction. The shape was large, menacing—and glowing. Every muscle in her body stiffened. Her heart pounded in her chest until she was dizzy.

She reached out and clung to Garrett's jacket with one hand, and pointed with the other.

With a shaky voice she said, "Garrett. I see a gh-ghost!"

Chapter Four

The figure drifted between the trees and seemed to float over the ground. The light outside Granny's room didn't quite reach the edge of the woods, and the moon was partially covered by a large cloud. The figure moved down the short incline from the woods.

Paige's heart pounded so loudly in her chest, the sound echoed in her ears.

"Paige," Garrett said. "Ghosts don't carry jugs of moonshine and a lantern."

The figure began to whistle, then sauntered into the light and waved. No ghost. Just Booker Vee.

Paige released a long, slow sigh. "Thank heavens."

"Paige," Garrett said, "you're really letting this whole ghost thing get to you." He faced her and stared into her eyes. "I'll prove to you that there are no ghosts."

"How?" she asked.

"We'll spend the night together in the mansion. In fact,

I'll move in and stay there until I get it fixed up. That way
I can prove to you, and the entire town, that the Taylor
mansion is just what it's supposed to be—empty."

"We?"

"It's the best way for you to get over your fears," Garrett
said.

"And there's no other reason you want me to spend the
night?"

He tilted his head. "Such as?"

"Come on, Garrett. From the start you've accused
Granny of inventing this entire story. And I'm sure you
suspect me as well. Are you hoping to catch me or Granny
in the act?"

"Are you saying I might catch either one of you in the
act?"

"No. You'd be wasting your time."

He grinned. "Prove it. Spend the night. If I'm with you
and something happens, I'll know that you had nothing to
do with it."

"And my grandmother?"

"She's another story." He rubbed his chin, the lack of
razor evident by the chafing sound. "So what do you say?"

"No. Yes. No. You're getting me confused." Paige
watched Booker enter Granny's apartment. In the window
she could see the hazy light in the room and could almost
smell the thick, heavy cigar smoke. She didn't relish the
idea of breathing in stale second-hand smoke all night. Her
attention returned to Garrett. "And where exactly would I
sleep?"

"Anywhere you'd like. I could make a few suggestions—"
He lifted his brows, a wicked grin forming on his mouth.

Paige couldn't keep from laughing. "I'm sure you
could." The idea of being in Garrett's arms all night

sounded nice, much too nice. Darn. He was doing it again, charming her into his web. She shrugged, not wanting to act too eager to sleep under the same roof with him. "Okay. But if anything happens, I'll—"

He moved closer and closer to her until his mouth was inches from hers. His voice lowered. "You'll what?"

Paige had to tilt her head back to meet his gaze. She caught a scent of his aftershave. Musk. That fit him. Manly. Seductive.

"Come on," he said. "I want to hear this McCormick threat. You've always acted so tough and still do. But I suspected then what I know now: You have a soft side to you. You're all woman, Paige. I don't buy your threats."

"I haven't threatened you, yet."

"Yet?" He waited for her reply as if anticipating the challenge.

She backed away. "I'll be over in a couple of hours. By then I should have a good threat for you."

"I'm looking forward to hearing it," he said.

Paige turned her back to him and headed for Granny's apartment, unable to suppress her involuntary smile.

Garrett wondered if he should have invited Paige to spend the night. She tempted him a little too much for his liking. But he needed to know for sure if she had anything to do with these so-called hauntings. If something happened tonight, he could cross Paige off his short list, and then that would narrow it down to one person, Moonshine McCormick.

Garrett wasn't quite sure why it was so important to him to know for sure if Paige had any involvement with the haunting of the Taylor mansion. Maybe he had to assure himself that she wasn't that devious, that manipulative. He hated to lump Paige in with the rest of the McCormick gang, but what else could he do? The family was known for twisting situations to their advantage at the expense of others.

The doorbell rang, drawing Garrett out of his thoughts. When he opened the door, Paige stood there with a sleeping bag tucked under her arm, and an overnight bag in her hand. She eyed him cautiously.

"Come in. Let me take your things." Garrett set her belongings in the parlor. All the sheets covering the furniture had been removed, and a nice, warm fire burned in the fireplace. The wind howled through the trees, and rustled the bushes that grew next to the house. "Sounds like it's going to be a stormy night."

"Yeah." Paige crossed the threshold and shoved the door shut behind her. She seemed nervous, awkward, on edge.

"Everything okay?" Garrett asked.

"Yes." She shrugged.

Garrett wondered if her mood didn't have something to do with dear old Granny. Maybe Granny planned to haunt the house tonight. The old woman couldn't have picked a better night for it, with the wind whistling, thunder booming, and lightning flashing.

"Has it started to rain yet?" Garrett asked.

"No. But it'll be here soon." Paige stuck her hands in her jeans pockets and looked around, clearly a little nervous. "Something smells good," she said.

"I thought you might be hungry, so I ran over to Mabel's Diner."

"Mabel's can rival some of the best restaurants in Oregon."

Garrett led the way into the dining room and held Paige's chair out for her, then poured the wine. He lifted the lid and steam rose from a pot of stew, the aroma making his stomach growl. After he dished up their plates, he handed her a biscuit.

"This room is so beautiful," Paige said. "I bet you had many dinners in here with your grandparents."

"Yes, I did." The thought warmed Garrett's heart.

"I just don't know how you could ever sell this place."

He sighed. "Here we go again. Why don't you give this up?"

She kept a steady gaze on him. "I was about to say the same thing to you."

"I'm doing what's best for everyone concerned."

"How can you say that? This mansion should stay in your family. A Taylor should always own the *Taylor* mansion." She sipped her wine.

"I have no one to pass it on to." He gulped his wine, then poured another glass for himself. This subject made him edgy. He wished she would drop it, but she was a McCormick, and McCormicks never dropped anything until they got what they wanted.

"Someday you will. And someday you'll regret selling it," Paige said.

Garrett changed the subject. "Do you plan on having a family some day?"

The thought made her smile. "Yes. I'd like children."

"How about a husband?" Garrett grinned and winked at her.

"Why, are you offering?" Paige laughed, then returned her attention back to her food.

He could tell she wasn't the teasing type, yet here she was flirting with him. That thought pleased him. "What would you say if I was?" Garrett asked.

She stopped chewing and looked at him, then forced a laugh. "Very funny."

Garrett wasn't even sure himself if he was kidding. For some unknown, crazy reason, marriage to Paige sounded right, felt right. But marriage? What was he saying? Maybe the house was haunted and his grandfather was putting words in his mouth. God knew, Grandpa had always wanted him to get married and carry on the Taylor name.

Even though his grandfather had never talked about it, Garrett suspected Rocky had felt he'd failed with Garrett's father, Milton. Garrett wasn't sure why his father had turned out the way he had, always on the move for a new deal, focused only on making more and more money, and so critical of his own wife and son that nothing was ever good enough.

Then his mother's constant neglect, keeping herself busy in one club or party after another, never finding time for her own son. Later in life, Garrett realized she had only been escaping her husband's constant belittling and put-downs.

That was when his grandparents had stepped in and had taken Garrett out of his parents' home and into their own. His parents hadn't had a choice. Social services had threatened to remove Garrett.

Perhaps his parents' lifestyle had been a blessing in disguise. Because without it, he would never have gotten to live with his grandparents, and those times had been the best days of his life.

Paige narrowed her stare at him, suspicion written all over her face. "What if I accepted your proposal?"

"Then we'd get married. I'm a man of my word."

"Hmm." Paige rested her elbow on the table and tapped her finger on her cheek. "Interesting. A Taylor marrying a

McCormick. You know, everyone in town would suspect we *had* to get married."

"Would that bother you?"

She lifted her shoulders. "No." She finished her biscuit, then said, "If I accepted your proposal, would you still sell the mansion?"

"Yes."

"Sorry, then. The deal's off." The tone of her voice indicated she was making light of the conversation.

Garrett wondered just how far Paige would go to save the museum and secure her grandmother's room and board. He had the feeling he would find out, sooner or later.

Paige had to admit she'd agreed to spend the night in the mansion because she had been curious to know what Garrett was up to. Maybe he thought his charm would make her spill the beans about Granny haunting the mansion. Of course, that was impossible since Paige herself wasn't sure if Granny was involved. She hoped she could learn more about whether Garrett had struck a deal with Lester and, if so, what it entailed. Maybe she could still talk Lester out of buying the place. After all, nothing was in writing, yet.

But if this deal went through, Paige didn't have to be a genius to figure out that the museum and Granny were in deep trouble. The lease agreement had been between Rocky and Granny, not the developer, which meant it would be up to Garrett to stand up for her grandmother and the museum. Fat chance of Garrett helping Granny out.

Lester probably knew his legal way around complications, anyway. And, make no mistake about it, Granny was a complication.

Granny's unpredictable living arrangements made it even more important for Paige to save the mansion.

Garrett was bound and determined to sell his grandfather's home, and prove Granny was the ghost. Would Granny go that far? The museum had become her life, and a studio in the mansion was her home. Granny would do just about anything to keep her room and board because she had no other place to go. Living with one of her friends would make her feel like a charity case, something that would just about tear up Granny inside.

Paige remained deep in thought throughout the rest of the meal, receiving only occasional glances from Garrett.

After dinner, Paige helped Garrett clean up; they then went into the parlor. Two sofas faced each other, with a coffee table between them. Garrett claimed one sofa and propped his feet up on the coffee table.

Paige put some distance between them by choosing the sofa across from him. What was it about him that drew her like a bee to honey? She knew it was more then just a physical attraction. He demonstrated qualities that were important to her, like honesty, intelligence, integrity, and compassion. He knew right from wrong.

"You're sure quiet tonight," Garrett said.

"I have a lot on my mind."

"Have you found out anything about the urn yet?"

"I wish I had." Paige's heart felt heavy. "The sheriff wasn't very helpful."

"He probably doesn't know what to do. This town's been practically crime-free, except for . . ." A long uncomfortable pause followed.

"Except for my father," Paige finished for him.

His mouth opened and closed. At first she thought he was going to deny that's what he meant. Then he said, "I'm sorry."

The lights flickered, causing both Paige and Garrett to

glance at the lamps near the sofas. A strong gust shook the window.

"That's not a ghost," Garrett said. "It's the wind. Hear it out there?"

"I hope you're right." Paige snatched a sofa pillow and hugged it.

"This mansion isn't haunted." Garrett spoke with confidence.

Paige wanted to believe him. More than that, she wanted to change the subject. "So, tell me what you did after you graduated from Patterson High School."

He shrugged. "I went to college, then after working a few years in a veterinary clinic in Eugene, I moved to Portland and started my own business. How about you?"

"You don't like talking about yourself, do you?" Paige asked.

"I'm pretty boring."

"You, boring? I don't think most women would agree with you." She keep a steady gaze on him, watching for his reaction.

He smiled. "Maybe years ago, but not now."

"Why do you say that?"

"My work isn't exciting. Not like yours," Garrett said.

"Hardly. It's hard work. Very little glamour, like most people assume there is. The toughest part about my job is the constant traveling. When I started out, I thought it was exciting. My first job out of college was working for a travel magazine. Since then, I've never been in the same place for very long, always moving, always on the go. It's getting old."

"Are you thinking of changing your career?" Garrett asked.

"Possibly."

"Would you settle in Oregon?"

Paige glanced into the fire. "If I did, it wouldn't be in Patterson. But I would like to live closer to my grandmother." Paige's mind raced. Somehow she needed to change the subject to the mansion. Nothing like the direct approach. "So when did you say the developer was returning?"

A slow, lazy smile spread on Garrett's mouth. He studied her before he spoke. "A month. Worried?"

"So you've negotiated a deal?"

"Inquisitive, aren't we?" He leaned forward, dropping his feet firmly on the floor, his elbows resting on his knees. "Would you like a glass of wine?"

Paige nodded. After Garrett stepped out of the room she gazed back into the fire. He was sure being evasive about the developer. Which told her he didn't have a deal yet. Otherwise, he would be gloating.

Garrett returned with two glasses and a new bottle of red wine. He poured hers full and handed it to her.

"Are you trying to get me drunk?" Paige said.

Raised brows accompanied his devilish grin. "Maybe I am." He returned to the sofa and settled before he poured himself a glass and lounged back. "You ever been married?"

"No. How about you?" Paige asked.

"Nope. You could say I've been married to my work." Garrett propped his feet back on the table. Despite his languid pose, Paige detected a tension in his rigid muscles. Was it the subject or company that made him uneasy? He closed his eyes and yawned. "It's been a long day."

"Why don't we call it a night?" Paige asked.

"Sounds good to me," Garrett said.

"Where should I throw my sleeping bag?"

"Wherever you want."

"How about here?" She patted the cushion she sat on.

"That's fine."

She eyed him. "And where are you going to sleep?"

"I guess right here." He pointed to the sofa he sat on.

Paige unrolled her sleeping bag while Garrett spread out a blanket. Garrett set a flashlight on the floor next to him, and then they snuggled into their makeshift beds.

Paige closed her eyes, hoping sleep would come quickly. Even though she was tired, her muscles were tense. The idea that the mansion might be haunted terrified her. She thought about keeping the light on all night. Ghosts couldn't appear if the room was lit, right? She hesitated. Garrett would undoubtedly think she was a coward, which she was when it came to spooky things. She couldn't even watch horror movies, because it left her with nightmares for weeks.

Paige gazed at the ceiling, trying to steady her rapidly beating heart, and listened to every sound: the fire crackling, the wind blowing, Garrett breathing. Every creak of the house made her muscles rigid. If Rocky Taylor was haunting the mansion, why now? He had been dead for well over a year. And what if the ghost wasn't Rocky, but an angry spirit of the past? Her mind whirled with outrageous possibilities, each striking more fear.

What would she do if a ghost appeared? She couldn't shew it away like a pesky fly. Did ghost-busters, exterminators of the dead, really exist? The more she let her imagination run wild, the more frightened she became, and the faster her pulse raced.

"Uh, Garrett," she whispered. "Garrett. Are you awake?"

"Huh?" He sounded half asleep.

Pride or no pride, she needed a light on. "Could you please turn on the lamp?"

"Why?"

"I can't sleep without it on."

He mumbled something incoherent before he lumbered off the sofa as if he had to will himself to do it, flipped the light on, then flopped back on the couch. "Happy now?"

"Yeah." Within minutes she could hear him go back to sleep as if he hadn't a care in the world. Obviously, he really didn't believe in ghosts, but Paige wasn't as convinced. In her opinion, too many people in town had heard sounds coming from the mansion. Granny was convinced it was Rocky Taylor even though she had never seen him herself. Paige didn't think Rocky would intentionally hurt her, yet she still didn't like the idea of a dead person appearing before her, or worse yet, glowing in front of her like a pumpkin on Halloween night.

She opened her eyes and glanced over at Garrett, sleeping like a baby. Captivated, she watched him. His nose was straight and strong, his jaw and cheekbones had the bone structure of a male model, his face was perfect. But what she really liked about him was his tenderness. His touch made her feel as if she were the only woman on the face of the earth he cared about, he wanted to be with, he wanted to love. Then there was his passion, hidden in his explosive kisses and touches.

He was a good man, a kind man. Deep down, Garrett reminded her of his grandfather, albeit a little quicker tempered. Garrett wouldn't talk about the nice deeds he had done for people, especially when it came to free veterinary care, but the folks in town talked. Even Granny had mentioned that Garrett had helped out several dairy farmers who couldn't afford an animal doctor's fee.

For some reason, knowing that about Garrett was important to Paige. She wanted to know, needed to know he would give to others, to lend a hand to someone in need.

Garrett was definitely Rocky's grandson. So why couldn't he help out the museum and Granny? Why was Garrett in such a hurry to get rid of the place? Money wasn't an issue, not for Garrett. Rocky had left him millions.

Something didn't make sense.

Too bad they were on opposite sides. Otherwise, she would have liked to have known him better, and sample a few more, no, a lot more of his kisses. But Granny came first. Family always did, which meant getting closer to Garrett was out of the question. A twinge of disappointment niggled at her.

The lamp suddenly flashed off.

Paige gasped, her stare fixed on the lamp, its red and gold shade barely visible in the dark. Her heart pounded. She was sure Rocky would appear any moment. Wouldn't that be her luck to have Garrett sleep through the entire ordeal?

"Garrett," she said in a strained whisper. "Garrett, are you awake?" When he didn't answer, she said his name louder.

He turned over, his back to her now.

Good grief, he was harder to wake up than the dead! "Garrett!"

He looked over his shoulder. "Did you say something?"

Paige sighed in frustration. "The lamp just went out by itself." She couldn't keep the panic out of her voice.

"I'm sure it's nothing."

Bang! Bang!

"What's that?" Paige said breathlessly. Her heart

pounded like a sledge hammer in her chest. "Garrett, go see what that noise was."

He rolled over on his back and looked at her. She couldn't tell what kind of expression was on his face, but she sure could guess what he was thinking about her. Crazy. Insane. Paranoid. Those were a few words that came to mind—and most likely his too.

The noise sounded again. This time Paige jumped up, hurried over and tugged on Garrett's arm. "Come on."

He slowly ambled to his feet, and snatched the flashlight, switching the light on. "You know. You really are a chicken."

"Call me all the names you want, just find out what that noise was." Paige followed behind Garrett on his heels. With her fist clenched at her side, she resisted clutching his shirt.

He halted and whirled around. "Why are you following me so closely?"

"I . . . I thought I could help." Paige wouldn't tell him the real reason was because she didn't want to be left alone in the parlor.

"Help? You're practically riding my back." He took a couple of steps, then stopped again. He raised his voice, sounding exasperated. "What exactly am I looking for?"

"Lower your voice," Paige said.

"Or what? The ghost will hear me?" Garrett chuckled. He inched across the foyer into his grandfather's study, beaming the light around the room.

"You know," Paige said in a breathless yet accusing tone, "it was your idea to stay here overnight."

"And it was quite brilliant. Wouldn't you say?"

"Brilliant? Staying in a ghost-infested house? If you ask me, it was the stupidest idea I've ever heard of."

"Then why'd you come?" Garrett moved the curtain to one side and looked behind it, then out the window. He crossed the room to the other set of drapes, that when opened, viewed the front yard. He kept the flashlight pointed at the floor while he grappled for the pull cord.

Paige followed him, but kept several steps back. "I'm really wondering that myself right now," she whispered.

Garrett rested his hand on the cord and glanced over his shoulder at her. "Come on, Paige. What's there to be afraid of?" He yanked on the cord, and in one swoosh drew the curtains wide. He kept his gaze on her while he spoke.

Paige's stare zeroed in on the window, and the illuminated face peering in. She felt as if someone knocked the wind out of her. She couldn't breathe, let alone speak, so she pointed, her mouth opening and shutting before a scream ripped from her throat. She ran to the front door, yanking it open and wanting to run far away.

A shadowy figure filled the door frame.

Another scream escaped Paige before all she saw was black.

Hearing Paige collapse on the floor, Garrett rushed over to her. "Paige, are you all right?" He knelt beside her and patted her face to revive her.

"I'm sorry about that, Garrett. We didn't mean to scare anyone. We got a call to check out the mansion," Deputy Dave said. "The caller said one of the lines running to your house is hanging close to the front window. We thought we'd better check it out, in case it started a fire."

Garrett wondered who might have called, but pushed that thought to the back of his mind, and attended to Paige.

"You want me to fetch the doctor?"

Garrett glanced at Deputy Dave, wearing his black rain

gear and holding a large flashlight, training the beam of light on Paige. "No. Thanks. I can handle things here,"

Deputy Dave nodded.

The sheriff soon joined him. "I don't see anything that could cause problems. The line down looks like cable. It can wait until tomorrow. Sorry for bothering you." Sheriff Raymond frowned, noticing Paige for the first time. "She okay?"

"She's fine. I'll take care of her." After the sheriff and deputy left, Garrett slammed the door. He lifted Paige into his arms and carried her to the sofa, setting her down gently.

She opened her eyes, confused and disoriented. "Wh-What happened?"

"You fainted."

Paige briefly closed her eyes. "I've never fainted before."

"There's a first time for everything. Now, let me examine you. You might have a concussion." He ignored her protest and checked her head, detecting a slight lump forming. "I'll get ice." With long strides, he swiftly covered the footage between the parlor and kitchen. He gathered ice in a plastic bag and returned, applying it to the back of her head.

"Why is it I'm always getting hurt when I'm around you?" Paige asked.

"Just lucky, I guess." Garrett pushed the table out of the way, then arranged the sofas together.

"Lucky?"

"Yes. If you weren't hurt, we couldn't play doctor."

She groaned, then narrowed her gaze at him. "What are you doing?"

"This way I can keep a closer eye on you in case your concussion is worse than it looks," he said, as he climbed onto the couch, pulling the blanket over him.

"The only thing worse than it looks around here is this house."

"Here we go again."

"And again. And again. What was that scary creature at the door?"

Garrett belly laughed before he said, "Deputy Dave." He dramatically sucked in a breath, then sarcastically said, "Boy, he is scary! Don't worry. I'll protect you from him."

"What was he doing here?" He could hear the annoyance in her voice, which made Garrett grin.

"A tree blew over onto some power lines. Which explains why the lights went out."

"Then what was the banging noise?"

Garrett's widened his eyes. "It was my grandfather rattling his chains."

"Very funny."

He tried but couldn't suppress the chuckle. "A loose cable. I'll take care of it tomorrow. Now, can we go to sleep?"

"I have to sleep with an ice bag on my head all night?"

"Wouldn't be a bad idea." He shifted to get more comfortable.

"I think you're the one that needs the ice on his head, coming up with this great idea to spend the night here." She folded her arms over her chest and stared at the ceiling.

Garrett smiled, and closed his eyes. He had her riled. And for some reason that really pleased him. "You whine an awful lot. You know that?"

"Well, you snore."

He blinked his eyes open and rolled his head to the side to look at her. "I do not."

"Okay. You don't. But you're hardly perfect."

He closed his eyes again, and felt sleep begin to over-come him, releasing a long yawn. In a groggy voice he said, "No, I'm not, but I think you're about as perfect as a woman gets."

A hush settled over the room.

The next morning, Paige met Granny in the museum. Granny kept busy rearranging books on the shelf of the museum store, and never asked Paige where she had been all night. A couple of local people milled around looking through the museum.

Slow again. When wasn't it?

That was the problem. They had one month to turn a profit, and one month wasn't very long, especially consid-ering the place had never made money since it opened. Somehow they had to drum up business. They needed peo-ple, in record numbers, to visit the museum. How? Paige knew that would take nothing short of a miracle.

"Since it's slow right now, I'm going to go into town and look around," Paige said.

Granny nodded. She was probably thinking about the museum, having one month to turn a profit, and the clock ticking away.

Paige negotiated her way through debris of limbs and leaves left in the wake of the storm. The Taylor mansion's grounds looked more like Mother Nature's war zone than the manicured landscaping she remembered.

The sound of chain saws roared as several men cut the fallen limbs and trees into smaller chunks. Earlier, Paige had spotted Garrett among the group working to clean up the mess, but she didn't see him now.

A strong aroma of fir, cedar, and sawdust assailed her

sense of smell, a scent that reminded Paige of hiking in the woods after a good rainfall.

She jogged across the street and headed for the jailhouse. She hadn't wanted to tell Granny that she intended to check into the urn investigation. Days had passed since the robbery, and Paige hadn't heard a word from the sheriff or deputy. So she decided to go to them. Maybe today wasn't the best day to ask, but she didn't want to wait any longer. Patience wasn't one of her virtues.

Paige entered the jail to find Deputy Dave asleep in his chair, his head tipped back and mouth wide open. He didn't hear the door shut, or her footsteps cross the office to his desk. She cleared her voice.

Deputy Dave snorted in a gulp of air, stirred in his chair, then went back to breathing deeply.

"Deputy Dave," Paige said softly. No response. She repeated his name a little louder. When he still didn't wake, she shouted, "Deputy Dave!"

He jolted to an upright position. Even though his eyes were open wide, he appeared bewildered. "Uh, what . . . who . . . what do you want?"

"Remember me? I'm Paige McCormick. I'm here to inquire about the robbery."

"A robbery? When and where did this happen?" Now alert, Deputy Dave clambered to his feet and shuffled over to where his gun belt hung on a hook. He latched the belt around his narrow hips, then drew his gun. With one hand, he felt for bullets in his shirt pocket. "Now where'd I put those?"

"They're on your gun belt," Paige said. "You don't need your gun. You've already investigated the robbery."

Deputy Dave held up his hand to silence her. "Hold on.

I can only do one thing at a time. Can't listen to you when I'm loading my gun." He picked several bullets off his belt.

"Those bullets are green," Paige exclaimed. "They're moldy."

"It's tarnish."

"Tarnish?"

"They haven't been used in awhile."

That was an understatement. "Will they even work?" Paige watched him place a bullet in the chamber.

"I guess we'll find out."

Sheriff Raymond opened the door and paused. "What on earth are you doing, Dave?" he exclaimed.

"This young gal said there's been a robbery." He jerked the nose of his gun toward Paige.

"We already investigated that. Put that gun away, and be sure to take the bullets out." Sheriff Raymond trudged to his desk and deposited himself in the chair. Black bags sagged under his eyes and the wrinkles on his face appeared more pronounced. He removed his hat, ran his fingers through his thinning gray hair, and released a weary sigh. "Now what can I do for you, young lady?"

"I came here to find out what progress you've made on the investigation of the urn stolen from the museum."

Sheriff Raymond shuffled papers on his desk while mumbling about being too busy for her questions. He picked a sheet up with notes on it and read it to himself. "Let's see here. We asked around town, but no one saw anything. We inspected the museum, but discovered nothing." He looked at her, a blank expression on his face.

"That's it?"

"I'm afraid so."

Paige couldn't believe it. Her family heirloom. The urn that was so near and dear to all the McCormicks was gone, and no one cared enough to find it. "Did you look in the woods?"

"I'll check it out, but I doubt a thief would stash a gold urn in the woods. He'd be more likely to sell it on the black market, or melt it down."

Nausea surged in Paige's stomach. Could anyone be so cruel as to do that? Growing up, especially when she had been ridiculed by other kids, she'd always had that story of the urn to hold on to, to lend her some dignity, some pride. Now the urn could be gone forever. She felt as if a part of her had been stolen along with it. She swallowed, hoping to rid herself of the tightening in her throat.

"Look at the bright side," Sheriff Raymond said. "Your grandmother will collect a bundle from the insurance company. Might even be enough for her to live her remaining years out on. Good always comes out of every bad thing that happens."

"Do you intend to do anything more?"

Sheriff Raymond lifted his shoulders and grimaced. "I'll put some calls in and do a little more checking on the computer. If anything comes up, I'll let you know. Now, you go on and stay out of trouble. I've got work to do. The storm's left this town in shambles, if you haven't noticed."

Paige clenched her fists and hurriedly left the jailhouse. It took her several controlled breaths to calm down. Looking for the urn was definitely not high on their priority list. Paige couldn't sit around and do nothing. She would search for the missing urn herself.

Instinct told her the urn was still in town. Or was that wishful thinking? No matter what, she intended to find that precious hunk of metal, if it was the last thing she did.

Crossing the road, Paige strolled down the street, deep

in thought. If no clues were found inside the museum, maybe she needed to retrace the thief's steps outside.

When Paige reached the mansion, she rounded the house to the back door of the museum and searched the ground for clues. Any clue would do. A dropped item, footprint, a ripped piece of material, anything—all of which were probably blown away by the storm.

Paige didn't see anything outside the museum door except for fir tree branches, maple leaves, and mud puddles. She had seen the thief dash away using a path that led from the back of the mansion and into the woods. Paige had never followed this path before. She had never had a reason to, until now.

The path started out flat, then meandered up a gentle incline. Granny went this way all the time. Somewhere deeper in the woods, the path led to her still where she made moonshine.

The canopy of the trees couldn't hide the fury the storm had left in its wake, evident by the broken limbs covering much of the trail.

Paige carefully made her way deeper into the woods until the path forked. She took the less-used path, because she knew the worn one led to Granny's still.

The trees began to thin out. Paige finally reached a clearing with a modern brown house, paved driveway, green lawn, and a red van parked out front. She searched the area for the owner and didn't have to wait long before two people came out of the house and strolled out onto the driveway.

Paige sucked in a breath, immediately recognizing Garrett. He was with a woman, a very attractive woman with short auburn hair and lovely makeup, wearing a navy blue tailored suit that shouted success.

Paige felt a stab of jealousy. The mere fact that she felt anything at all angered her even more. She didn't want to feel any emotions, because that meant Garrett was breaking down her wall and getting much too close.

The woman climbed in the van and started the engine. Garrett waved, then turned in Paige's direction.

Quickly, Paige hid behind a pile of dead logs, crouching out of sight. The last thing she wanted was for Garrett to think she was following him. She held her breath when Garrett strode by, following the trail back to the mansion. She waited for him to disappear from sight, and for the woman to drive away, before she came out of hiding.

Nearing the house, she looked around for anyone else who might be living there, or visiting, but there was no one, not even a dog or cat.

Paige paused at the garage. Could this woman have stolen the urn? And how did she know Garrett? Could she be his girlfriend? Lover?

Paige glanced back at the path. This woman would have had easy access to the mansion without being seen. Also, she could have been watching the museum to see when the opportune time would be for a robbery.

Paige decided to investigate the garage. It had a large window on one side, but it was too high for Paige to look in. So she pulled over an aluminum garbage can, climbed up and peered in. The dim interior of the garage couldn't conceal the many pieces of antique furniture and items that filled the space.

Paige sucked in a breath.

This woman had to be the thief who stole her family's urn! Could all the items in the garage be stolen too? Did Garrett know about this? Was he involved? What was his connection to this redhead?

Paige pressed her forehead against the window and cupped her hands on each side of her face to cut the glare of light. She scanned the inside of the garage, but didn't see the urn, yet it had to be in there. Maybe the woman had hidden it inside a cabinet. No one would keep something that valuable in plain sight.

Paige pushed on the window, but it wouldn't budge. She would break the window if she had too. With more effort, she tried again. This time, it cracked ajar. She opened it wide, then grasped the window ledge, and hopped up, like a gymnast on the parallel bars, bracing her hips between her hands. She looked around for something to grab onto, but there was nothing within reach. So she would have to slide forward on to the concrete floor. With her upper body leaning forward, her legs and feet dangled in the air, Paige reached for the ground, but her jeans pocket snagged on the window frame.

Great!

She wiggled her hips to free herself.

"What do you think you're doing?" a deep voice demanded.

Chapter Five

Paige gasped. How would she ever explain this one? And her name being McCormick wouldn't help, no matter what her excuse was.

She grunted as she lifted her body up, then settled her feet back on the garbage can, her face flushed and breathing labored. "I can explain."

"What are you up to?" Garrett demanded.

She jumped down from the garbage can, then crossed her arms over her chest. "I'm looking for the urn. You haven't seen it lately, have you?"

His glare narrowed on her. "Are you accusing me of stealing it?"

"Maybe not you, but your lady friend just might have lifted it." Darn, she sounded jealous. Worse yet, she felt jealous.

"That 'lady friend' is my cousin, Jeannie Nelson, and *she* didn't steal anything."

Paige expelled a sharp breath. "Have you looked in her garage? It's full of antiques."

Garrett folded his arms over his chest. "She's an antique dealer. I just helped her unload."

"And?" Paige clamped her hands on her hips.

"And what?" Garrett's nostrils flared.

"Did you find my stolen urn?"

"I can't believe, you of all people, are accusing *my* family of stealing."

Her head tilted back, his words hitting harder than any punch ever could. "Oh, yes. I forgot how squeaky clean the Taylor family was." She shook her head in disgust, but kept her voice calm. "One person in my family made mistakes. Don't categorize all of us." She charged passed him, fighting tears of frustration.

Garrett reached out and grabbed her by the arm.

She halted but wouldn't look at him.

"Paige . . . I'm sorry." His words sounded forced.

She jerked her arm free. "Leave me alone." As she stormed away she could feel Garrett watching her until she disappeared from his view. His words cut deep, deeper than she would care to admit to. At the same time, Garrett reminded her how some things never change. She was a McCormick. He was a Taylor. The two didn't mix. She had to forget about Garrett and focus on Granny and the urn.

Paige wondered if the stolen urn and hauntings were related. Other than both incidents happening at the mansion around the same time, she didn't see another connection at this point.

Paige might have hit a dead end, but she didn't intend to give up. Too much was at stake.

She trudged into the museum, feeling depressed.

"What's wrong?" Granny asked. "You look upset."

"In a word, Garrett," Paige said.

Granny's voice dropped to a whisper. "I keep telling you to stay away from that boy. He's trouble."

Paige frowned. "Why are you whispering?"

Granny jerked her head to one side, and darted her eyes in the same direction.

Paige immediately spotted Garrett's mother, Anne Taylor. She was a nice-looking woman in her mid-fifties with short strawberry blond hair, and never a lock out of place. Her clothes were always coordinated, and her makeup expertly applied. Her small size contrasted with Garrett's tall frame. She was a quiet woman who kept mostly to herself.

Anne had remained in Patterson even after she and her husband had divorced nearly ten years ago. Paige wondered why Anne had remained in Patterson.

Anne was within hearing range, so Paige lowered her voice. "Maybe for once I'll listen to you. I think you're right. He is nothing but . . ." She glanced over at Granny, who appeared to be deep in thought with faraway glazed eyes. "Granny, are you listening? What's wrong?"

Snapping out of it, Granny shook her head. "Nothing."

"Nothing? You were a million miles away just a second ago."

Granny sighed, gave another glance to Anne, who had moved closer to them, then returned her attention to Paige. "I might as well tell you."

"Tell me what?" A knot formed in Paige's stomach.

"The insurance company isn't convinced the urn was stolen. They intend to investigate the situation themselves. It could take months before they can determine whether they'll pay up or not."

"What?" Paige replied in a strained whisper. "What do

they think? We stole the urn ourselves to collect the insurance money?"

Granny suddenly looked older, worry deepening the wrinkles on her forehead, around her eyes, and circling her clamped lips. She nodded.

"This is unbelievable."

"Lower your voice," Granny warned.

"No. I won't lower my voice. I can't believe the insurance company won't pay up. We've had insurance on that urn for more years than I care to remember." Paige realized just exactly what this meant. Without the insurance money, and in less than a month, Granny could have no home, no museum, and no money. Now Paige had one more reason to be angry with Garrett.

"This fight isn't over yet, Granny," Paige said with conviction. "We still have three and a half weeks."

"Look around. It wouldn't matter if we had one year to turn a profit," Granny said.

"Don't give up. Somehow, someway we will get this museum to turn a profit."

"Then what?" Granny looked dejected, defeated. "Wait for the developer to throw me out? He won't stick to his agreement."

Paige had the same thought, but kept it to herself. The situation seemed like a lost cause, but she refused to give up so soon, so easily. There had to be a way to save the museum and Granny from eviction.

There just had to be!

Saturday afternoon Paige spent much of the time wrapping Granny in gauze so she could go to the Halloween dance at the local grange as a mummy. Then Paige dressed up as a gypsy girl. She would share Lily's booth with her, taking turns telling fortunes and using Lily's crystal ball. Paige wasn't a psychic, and didn't have a clue of what to do or say. The booth was all in fun with the money being contributed to the museum, which wouldn't be much, but it was better than nothing.

Paige had borrowed her costume from Vivian. The silky red dress flared in the skirt, and a yellow sash tied at the waist. She wore large gold hoop earrings, a purple bandana around her forehead, and red high heels. Several people had already arrived at the dance by the time Paige and Granny entered the grange hall. Paige went directly to the booth.

"Sorry I'm late, Lily," Paige said. "It wasn't easy wrapping Granny. I think we bought the town out of gauze."

"No worry, dear. I've only had a few customers." Lily, dressed as a green-faced witch with a pointed hat, a black dress, and a large wart on her nose, left the booth and joined her friends gathered around the desserts.

Paige sat down at a small round table covered in a black cloth with yellow moons and stars on it, then waited for her first customer.

Jean shuffled over to the table, dropped several dollars into a donation jar, and then sat in a chair across from Paige.

"Do you want me to tell you what life holds for you?" Paige asked.

" 'Life's but a walking shadow, a poor player that struts and frets his hour upon the stage and then is heard no more, it is a tale told by an idiot, full of sound and fury, signifying nothing', " Jean quoted.

"Let me guess," Paige said. "Shakespeare's *The Tempest*."

"No," Jean said.

"Uh, *Hamlet*."

"No, no, no. It's *Macbeth,*" Jean said, smiling. "Now, tell me, what does my future hold?"

Paige ran her hands over the crystal ball. The surface was smooth and cool to her touch. She stared in it, wondering if anyone really saw something inside, because she didn't see anything except for the tablecloth magnified through the glass. "The spirits say that you will live a long, long life, and that you will win the big pot at next week's poker game."

"We are such stuff as dreams are made on and our little life is rounded with a sleep," Jean said.

"*Merchant of Venice,*" Paige exclaimed.

Jean shook her head. "You need to brush up on your Shakespeare. That was *The Tempest.*" She stepped to the flap opening and pushed the curtain aside, searching the room. "Ah, I see a young man, who appears to be looking for someone."

"Oh?" Paige tried to sound uninterested.

Jean glanced back at Paige, a gentle grin playing at the corners of her mouth. " 'But love is blind and lovers cannot see the pretty follies that themselves commit.' " She exited the tent, not waiting for Paige to guess what Shakespeare play she had just quoted from.

Paige contemplated the poetic words. Her feelings toward Garrett must be outwardly obvious. She felt like a fool. Before she could dwell on it, her next customer arrived.

Garrett's head almost hit the top of the tent. He wore an overcoat and puffed on an unlit curved pipe.

"Sherlock Holmes, I presume," Paige said, trying to act as if his presence didn't cause her heart to leap and pulse to race. Why'd he have to look so darn attractive, even in an overcoat, wearing a silly hat, and pretending to puff on an oversized pipe? And he smelled so good, clean, and freshly shaven.

His eyes studied her for a moment, drifting over her costume, then he lifted his brows. "You're smart for a gypsy girl." His voice came out deep, almost husky.

"I'm a woman, not a girl. Or haven't you noticed?"

"Oh, I've noticed all right." He sat across from her, his gaze never leaving her face. "So tell me, gypsy woman, what does my future hold?"

"My fee is a dollar a minute."

Garrett frowned. "I thought it was on donation."

"For you, it's a dollar a minute." Paige met him squarely in the eyes.

"I can see you're still angry with me." When she didn't reply, he said, "Okay. How long do you think you'll be at the dance tonight?"

Paige shrugged.

"Well, let's see. I'll buy two hours of your time." He pulled out his wallet and dropped several large bills into the bucket, then turned back to her. "Now you're mine for the next two hours."

"The money's for the reading, not me," Paige argued. The last thing she wanted was to be close to Garrett all night long. He made her nervous, and giddy. She couldn't think sensibly with him around. His mere presence made her go weak in the knees. And he had a way of making her forget that *he* was the enemy.

"And you think you can sit here and tell me my future for two hours?" Garrett asked, followed by a chuckle.

Ignoring his logic, she looked into the crystal ball. "I see you in the future keeping the mansion and letting the museum stay where it's at."

She wouldn't have known he heard her at all except for

the grin of annoyance on his face. He slid his hand over hers. His deep penetrating stare seemed to look right into her heart and soul.

And what would he find there? Paige wanted to believe he would find nothing but a casual interest, but she knew that to be false. Garrett stirred her senses, senses she didn't know she possessed until now, senses that made her feel alive and wanting more.

He removed his pipe, and then placed his elbows on the table, leaning close to her. "Tell me what you see for you and me, Paige. Because, dammit, I know we have a chemistry between us. I know you feel it too."

Oops. He did see into her heart.

She stared at the crystal ball to avoid looking into his eyes any further. "I see the woman of your dreams coming into your life and you will marry her and have a family."

"Is that woman you?"

"Garrett, I travel the world. My lifestyle doesn't permit me to have a relationship with anyone. Doesn't this costume say it all?"

"That's not what the costume says to me." He made no effort to hide the desire in his eyes.

A tingling sprang to life inside her, that feeling a young girl got each time she spotted her first love. Paige guessed maybe in high school she had felt that way. But it hadn't been toward Garrett. No. She had admired him from afar. Even then she had known he'd been way out of her league. She was a McCormick. In this town, people had made sure she had known her place.

When she met his comment with silence he said, "Doesn't that lifestyle get pretty lonesome, Paige? One of these days you're going to have to stop running."

"I'm not running." She sounded defensive.

"Yes, you are. You're running from your past, from Patterson, from your family, from your father."

"What do you know about it?" She clambered to her feet and maneuvered around the table to exit the tent.

Garrett grabbed her wrist and pulled her to him. "You're running again."

Paige averted her eyes to the ground.

"I thought I paid for a two-hour reading," Garrett said. Before she could answer his lips came down on hers, kissing her tenderly.

Paige fought for rationale to take control. Every time he held her in his arms and showered her with kisses, she melted just like butter on a hot day. This behavior was so unlike her. She controlled her destiny, and Garrett wasn't in her future. Her body eased when his hand wound around to her back and pulled her even closer to him. His heat penetrated right though the material of her costume. His touch was warm, comforting, and exciting.

The flap whipped open. A guy dressed as a rock star stood there. "Hey, I thought this booth was where you got your fortune read. But I'll settle for kissing."

"Buzz off, pal," Garrett said. "The gypsy woman's with me."

The guy slowly backed out, holding his hands up in surrender until the flap dropped closed.

"You're scaring my customers away."

"The only customer you have for the next two hours is me, remember?"

"That's fine, but I hope you realize the money I make tonight goes to the 'Save The Museum' fund."

"Really?" Garrett didn't sound too happy about that news.

"So what now?" Paige said.

He raised his brows as a wicked grin crossed his lips. "I could think of a few things, but nothing we could do here, so would you like to dance?" He motioned for her to lead the way, opening the flap for her.

As they stepped onto the dance floor Paige noticed many more people had arrived. She glanced around the room trying to spot anyone she recognized. Sheriff Raymond, dressed as King Arthur, danced with his wife, outfitted as Guinevere. Mayor Gunthrey came as a scarecrow, Barney Dowell wore a vampire costume, and the Butler brothers came, appropriately enough, as the Three Stooges.

Paige searched, but couldn't find Granny's whereabouts or any of her friends. Strange. They had been over by the dessert table just minutes before. Where could they have gone to?

Garrett twirled Paige around on the dance floor, waiting anxiously for a slow song to start, but each time a fast song came on, one after another. Dressed in her gypsy costume, Garrett had never seen a woman look more beautiful than Paige. She was now in his thoughts constantly, especially at night when he closed his eyes to sleep. But he didn't sleep. Visions of her appeared over and over in his mind.

He liked the contrasts in her personality: one minute angry and defiant, the next minute laughing and agreeable. Confident one moment, then vulnerable the next.

He couldn't deny the strong pull of his desires each time he looked at Paige. He didn't care that this woman complicated his life, and at the moment was on opposite sides of a very delicate matter from him, nor did he care that she was capable of wreaking havoc on his life. Was it instinct or pure love that was pushing him to seek her out, to be with her, to convince her they could have a relationship no matter what the circumstances were?

Garrett had never believed in chemistry between a man and woman. He had always thought that men and women had desires that fulfilled a need, whether it be physical or emotional, and that's what drove them to intimacy. But now he realized there could actually be more to a relationship. An electricity could occur between certain people. He didn't know how or why it existed. Did it matter?

Most important, he realized that an attraction this strong between a man and woman came along only once in a person's life. To capture this special magic—and keep it for a lifetime—was rare indeed.

Garrett lifted Paige's hand over her head and pirouetted her around. He had to brace himself every time they touched. The warmth from her skin literally shot heat to every part of his body. He felt more alive than he ever had in his life, and it felt good, too good to let go of.

A slow song began. Garrett didn't give her time to catch her breath. He pulled her close to him, and dragged in the scent of her perfume. He wanted to take his cape and wrap it around the both of them, and hold her forever.

"May I cut in?" Booker said, narrowing a challenging glare at Garrett.

Garrett felt irritation rise in his gut. This was his time with Paige, and he didn't want to share her with anyone. Using the good manners he had been taught, Garrett reluctantly stepped back.

Booker took Paige's hand, keeping a foot distance between them, and continued dancing slowly. He moved her toward the center of the floor, and then he chuckled. "I do believe I just pissed that boy off."

Paige smiled, and looked into Booker's face. "You want to know something else? He paid for a two-hour reading. I charged him a dollar a minute, and the money's going to the 'Save the Museum Fund' to keep it open."

Booker let out a whooping laugh. "Paige, you're wicked."

"Hey, I told him where the money was going."

They danced in silence for several minutes before Booker said, "Just look at him over there watching us like a coyote outside a chicken pen. I think that boy's got it bad for you."

"What do you mean?" Paige tried to ignore the excitement rushing through her, her breath suddenly quickening.

"That boy's in love with you. Can't you see that? Or maybe you just don't want to."

Booker was right. She didn't want to because then she would have to acknowledge her own feelings for Garrett, and they seemed to grow deeper as each day passed.

"Granny isn't gonna like this," Booker added.

"Speaking of Granny, where is she?" Paige glanced around the grange hall.

"I think she went back to her apartment with Jean. Her costume was unraveling. I'll go check on her in a minute. First I want to finish dancing with my favorite gal." He gave her a toothy grin.

Booker wasn't a good dancer, definitely not as smooth as Garrett. Several times Booker's large feet stepped on Paige's, but she bit her lower lip instead of saying anything. She knew he would never intentionally hurt her. His flipper-sized feet just got in the way sometimes, that's all.

When the song ended Booker gallantly bowed. "Thank you, ma'am."

"Thank you, kind sir." When Booker turned to leave Paige said, "Hey, Booker, why didn't you dress up?"

"I did." A big smile displayed his white teeth. "I'm dressed as a farmer." He hooked his large thumbs under the straps of his jean overalls.

"Booker, you *are* a farmer," Paige said.

"My boy runs the farm now. I mainly run my fix-it shop. I wear this for both jobs. So I have a year-round costume. Pretty handy, huh?" He laughed as he walked away, but when he reached Garrett, Booker's smile faded and eyes squinted in a sneer. They exchanged an unspoken warning, neither man backing down as they passed each other. Booker headed outside, disappearing behind the grange door.

Despite a fast song playing next, Garrett gathered Paige into his arms and kept their pace to a slow rhythm. "I don't think that man likes me much."

"Do you blame him? You're throwing his best friend out in the street."

"Please, for one night let's not talk about the museum, the mansion, and especially ghosts," Garrett said.

"Okay. Truce. No more for tonight, but I can't promise you what tomorrow will bring."

"Oh? So you're planning on seeing me tomorrow?" He pulled her closer and rested his cheek against her head.

They danced in silence. Paige could feel the muscles in Garrett's shoulders bend and flex with each movement to the music. His hand resting on her waist unconsciously tightened, then loosened. How could it feel so right to be in his arms?

They were on opposite sides of a serious situation that could escalate into war. Yet, feeling his breath stir the strands of her hair, his fingers intertwined with hers, their bodies swaying back and forth together, pressing so tight she could almost hear his heart beat, it almost seemed as if they had been together their entire lives. Garrett was one of those people she could have sworn she had known all her life, but hadn't. In fact in school they had never talked, not even a casual "hello."

She was surprised he had remembered her. Of course the McCormick name was infamous in this town.

"Hello, Garrett. Are you going to introduce me to your— friend?"

Paige took a step back and smiled at Anne Taylor, dressed as Queen Elizabeth. Anne seemed to fit the part of royalty, with her slim elegant stature and attractive face. She had always carried herself in a reserved and dignified manner. The years had been good to her.

"Mother, where have you been? You disappeared right after we came into the hall," Garrett said.

Anne frowned. "I've been here the entire time."

"I didn't see you."

"Perhaps your attention was on someone else." Anne glanced at Paige with a knowing smile. "My son is quite taken with you, and I can see why. You've turned into a beautiful woman, Paige."

"Thank you."

"And how is your grandmother coming along with the museum?"

"Struggling." Paige wasn't going to lie just to save Garrett from an awkward moment.

"I'm sorry to hear that. I was in there the other day and I meant to talk to her about the museum, but it didn't appear to be the right time." Her glance strayed to Garrett, then returned to Paige. "My son doesn't tell me much of what he's up to with the mansion these days."

A sudden tension arose between Garrett and his mother, but being trained in social graces, Anne merely smiled and acted as if nothing had happened.

"It was a pleasure to meet you," Anne said, touching Paige on the shoulder. "I'd love to have lunch together some time."

"I'd like that." Paige didn't expect to like Garrett's mother, but she did. Anne appeared to see Paige as a person, rather than a McCormick. Anne Taylor was much different than she had expected.

Garrett pulled her back into her arms, this time tighter, and closer, if that were possible.

"What was that all about?" Paige asked. She knew it was none of her business, but she just had to know. Curiosity hadn't killed her cat, Buster yet, so it couldn't hurt her either.

"Let's just say my mother and I don't see eye-to-eye on selling the mansion."

Paige stopped and pulled back. "Really?"

Garrett wouldn't elaborate on the subject. Paige didn't pry any further.

"Would you like a glass of punch?" Garrett asked, his mood suddenly cooled.

"Sure."

Before they reached the refreshment table, Booker burst through the doors, panting. "Rocky Taylor appeared in the window of the mansion," he shouted. "And the piano is playing like there's no tomorrow!"

Chapter Six

Gasps could be heard throughout the room. Then, in one mad rush, people ran out the door and headed for the mansion.

"Oh, great!" Garrett said. He glared at Paige. With long strides he hurried, then broke into a run.

As he neared, he could hear the piano blaring sullen music, like a scene straight out of a horror movie.

Garrett reached the mansion first and climbed the front steps, blocking the front door. "No one is going inside. You're trespassing and I want all of you to leave this minute."

Booker pushed his way to the front of the crowd. "Your grandpappy is trying to tell us something, and we should listen to him."

Garrett sighed. If he learned that Granny McCormick was behind this, he would wring her neck. That woman was a thorn in his side. She was the one who put these

103

ghost ideas in everyone's head. "There is no ghost, people. Now everyone go back to the dance."

"If there's no ghost, then who's playing the piano?" Booker challenged.

"It's playing by itself. It's a player piano that's malfunctioning. That's all."

"It's awfully coincidental that it malfunctions on a regular basis, and only started malfunctioning when you came to town." Booker stood his ground, the look on his face daring Garrett to argue the point.

Granny appeared beside Paige, voicing her opinion to the crowd. "It's the ghost of Rocky Taylor. I know it is. I hear him almost every night, and have ever since his grandson came to town."

Murmuring sounded throughout the crowd.

"Let us be the judges," Granny said. "Prove to us that it's the piano malfunctioning."

"No." Garrett's anger twisted a knot in his stomach. "I'm not about to let the entire town of Patterson traipse through my house when I'm trying to sell it."

"Then let a few of us go in," Booker said.

Sheriff Raymond made his way through the crowd and onto the porch, pinning his badge to his King Arthur costume. Deputy Dave, wearing Superman tights, cape, and a large "S" on his chest, joined the sheriff. Sheriff Raymond raised his hands and gestured for the people to calm down. "This is private property, people. If Garrett Taylor doesn't want anyone on this property, you'll all have to leave."

"Sounds to me like you're hiding something," Granny said. The townspeople murmured in agreement.

Garrett glared at Paige. Couldn't she keep that woman *quiet?* Granny, the bulldog, wouldn't let it go until she got her bone.

Paige shrugged. "It would get them off your back."

Garrett clenched his fists in frustration. "Okay. If everyone will leave afterwards, I'll let a handful of people check out the piano."

Booker climbed the porch. "I think Lily should be one of them. She's more knowledgeable about these kinds of things."

Lily stepped forward. Granny joined them, along with Paige, Booker, Sheriff Raymond, Deputy Dave, and Anne Taylor.

Just after they entered the house, Garrett pulled Paige aside. "If this crowd gets out of control I'll hold you responsible." A tension was suddenly between them.

Garrett regretted his words the second they flew out of his mouth. Darn, these McCormicks. They brought out the worst in him. If the grandmother wasn't driving him crazy with her ridiculous accusations, then Paige was taunting him with her full lips and big brown eyes.

Paige yanked her arm free and caught up to the group at the bottom of the stairs.

Garrett watched her hips as she walked away, her skirt swaying back and forth. Paige had him wrapped around her little finger. And he was powerless to do anything about it.

Garrett took several steps, when something in the parlor window caught his eye. Many of the townspeople peered in, their faces pressed against the glass, trying to get a better glimpse. Garrett shook his head. This kind of excitement would surely be the talk of the town for years to come.

Selling the mansion had been a headache from the start, and it was only getting worse. Garrett caught up to the group, led by Sheriff Raymond, and slowly climbed the stairs. Each deliberate step brought the music louder and closer. At long last they reached the top of the third floor.

The door to the music room was shut. The group gathered at the door.

Carefully Sheriff Raymond placed his slightly shaking hand on the knob and turned it. He pushed the door open and everyone filtered into the room, their stares directed at the player piano across the room. The music stopped. An eerie silence filled the room. The group exchanged nervous glances.

"I feel his presence," Lily whispered.

"What is he trying to tell us?" Booker asked in a soft voice.

Lily shook her head. "We'd have to have a seance to find that out."

"Good grief," Garrett exclaimed as he charged over to the piano. "The piano malfunctioned." He kicked the musical instrument, hoping it would turn on again. He tried again, kicking it harder, then again, but the piano remained silent. He whirled around and peered at each person present. "You can't possibly believe that my grandfather was playing this piano."

"He played it when he was alive," Anne said.

"Oh," Garrett said on a groan. "Not you too, Mother."

She shrugged. "I don't know. Maybe we should have a seance. If Rocky's here, then we can find out what's troubling him."

"As if we don't already know!" Granny said.

Great! Now his mother believed all this nonsense. He pulled his hat off and ran his fingers through his hair. All eyes were on him waiting for his answer. He met Paige's beautiful dark brown eyes, and silently pleaded for her to do something, anything. But there was nothing she could do. Only he could put an end to it.

"All right. We'll have a seance on one condition. That

afterward everyone drops this subject and leaves me and my house alone."

All heads nodded.

"Fair enough," Booker said.

The group traipsed back down the stairs, sounding like a herd of cattle.

"I'll tell the crowd what we're doing. Hopefully they'll leave," Sheriff Raymond said.

Garrett didn't count on it. "Why don't we go into the dining room?"

Anne led the way and flipped the light switch on, then adjusted the light to dim. She gestured for Lily to seat herself at the head of the table. Booker sat on one side of Lily, while Granny took the other side. Garrett sat beside his mother, and Paige sat next to Deputy Dave, across the table from Garrett.

Sheriff Raymond returned. "Most of the people are leaving. I'm returning to the dance. Seances aren't my cup of tea, especially on Halloween night. But you'll be in good hands with Deputy Dave, here." He waved, then left.

"I'll need my crystal ball," Lily said.

"I'll get it," Booker said, hurrying out of the house.

An awkward quiet engulfed the room. People around the table glanced at one another, but not much was said. Garrett tried to avoid looking at Paige, yet he found himself gazing at her several times, and then inwardly chastising himself for being so weak. He doubted he would ever get tired of admiring the curve of her face, her soft lips, and the smooth texture of her skin.

The last thing he had planned on doing this evening was sitting around a table with a bunch of people having a seance. His earlier hope—of bringing Paige back here, settling in front of a warm fire, opening a bottle of wine, and creating their own magic—had evaporated.

The front door slammed, rattling the house. Garrett jolted back to reality, his body going rigid. He could feel warmth rush to his face, and was grateful for the dimly lit room.

Booker set the crystal ball in front of Lily.

"Now, close your eyes and hold hands," Lily said. She dragged in a deep breath, exhaling in a rush, repeating the process several times. A long moment of silence followed. "Rocky Taylor. Do you hear us? Come to us, Rocky. Tell us what is troubling you . . ." Her voice trailed off. "If you are here, give us an indication."

Garrett looked at everyone at the table, their eyes closed tightly. Did they really believe this? He held back a chuckle.

Keys rattled under the table. Undoubtedly they belonged to Deputy Dave, whose legs were probably shaking like an earthquake, matching his trembling hands.

Suddenly, the window flew open and banged against the wall, inciting gasps from everyone at the table, their stares fixed across the room.

A bunch of snoopy townspeople gasped back at them. They looked as surprised at the window bursting open as the group inside the house did.

Garrett pushed out of his seat, crossed the room in three long strides, then secured the window, flipping the latch to a locked position. There. That won't happen again. He returned to his seat and scooted the chair in. "It was the people outside pushing on the window, hoping to get a better view," Garrett mumbled, feeling a need to say something.

"Shhh," Lily said, followed by a reprimanding glare from

Booker. Lily continued. "Now that we know you are here, tell us what is troubling you."

"Ask him if he's upset his grandson is selling the place," Granny said, then narrowed her eyes at Garrett.

Was he the only sane person at this table? The window opening wasn't his grandfather making his presence known, but nosey people trying to see what was going on. Lily and the others were grasping at straws. They wanted to believe in ghosts so badly they would take anything as a sign.

Okay. All he had to do was be patient. Once this farce of a seance was over, he could go back to fixing the place up—undisturbed! Everyone would leave him alone. After the month was over, and Granny failed to turn a profit, he could sell the place to Les. The house would be out of his hair, and no one would ever have to know about his family's past.

Mission accomplished!

"If the mansion being sold is what's troubling you, then give us another sign." Lily took a deep breath and exhaled slowly. "Tell us, Rocky."

Nothing happened.

Garrett felt like telling them, "I told you so." They sat there for what seemed like eternity. No object moved by itself, no sound could be heard in the house, and no ghostly figure appeared.

"Wait!" Lily said. "I hear him. He's saying he is angry, because he gave his grandson this house out of love. He says Garrett is desecrating his memory by selling the mansion."

"This is ridiculous," Garrett said, his patience near the breaking point. "She's making all of this up. You don't really believe she can hear my grandfather, do you?" Garrett glanced at each person at the table, staring back at him as if he were the one insane, not Lily. He forced out a breath. "Oh, come on!"

Everyone, even his mother looked convinced.

"Did anyone else besides Lily hear my grandfather speak?" Garrett's question was met with silence. He added, "I didn't think so."

"You must stop this nonsense," Granny said. "Stop the sale of the mansion."

"She's right," Lily added. "In order for your grandfather to leave this world and enter the beyond he must finish his business here. Only you can release your grandfather by complying with his wishes."

"Those wishes aren't my grandfather's. They're Moonshine McCormick's." He jabbed his finger in the air. "And all of you are helping her." Garrett stood so quickly his chair skidded out behind him. His back was against the wall, and he knew it. Their scheme wouldn't work. He had to think of his mother, even if she didn't know he was doing this for her. He couldn't risk the trauma she would experience if the town found out about their past.

"I've been very patient up to now. I've let you in my house, you've seen the music room, and I've even tolerated this seance. Now, I'm going to have to ask all of you to leave."

"Garrett," Anne said in a reprimanding tone.

"You too, mother. You can buy into this conspiracy, but I won't."

"You're being very rude," Anne said.

"And you're being very gullible. I have work to do. So you'll understand if you see yourselves out." Garrett charged out of the room, and out of the house, slamming the door behind him. He pushed through the people still waiting out front, and walked back to the front of the grange where he had left his truck. After climbing inside, he jabbed his key into the ignition, then sat there.

He pounded his hands on top of the steering wheel. Dammit. Why couldn't these people leave him alone? He just wanted to sell a house. What was so wrong about that? Most people would do the same if they were in his same situation. How dare those McCormicks try and pull a fast one on him. And they have the nerve to bring the townspeople in on their scheme. How naive did they think he was? He wouldn't fall for it. Not for one single minute.

Paige flitted in his mind. A sense of loss swept over him. He could have had something wonderful with her, but now it was too late. He couldn't trust her just as he couldn't trust her grandmother. Not once did she take his side. She had had ample opportunity.

This wasn't as easy for him as everyone thought. He was giving up a precious gift his grandfather had given him, something that represented everything about his family that he cherished. But he had no choice.

Common sense told him Moonshine McCormick was behind all of this. She had everything to lose. Well, to heck with all of them. He had to do what he had to do. He would sell the mansion, and that was that. End of discussion. As for Paige, well, maybe if things were different . . . Right now, the situation made it impossible for them to be anything more than acquaintances on opposite sides of the fence.

Pulling out of the parking lot, Garrett drove towards his farm house. Hopefully now he could fix the mansion up without being disturbed, then leave this town with his mother and never look back.

*   *   *

Paige picked up the ringing phone. "Hello?"

"Miss McCormick, this is Sheriff Raymond. I just wanted you to know that I checked on our police computer, hoping for any leads on the urn."

"And?"

"And nothing. I came up empty-handed. Sorry."

"What about the woods?" Paige asked. "Did you check behind the mansion?"

"Yes, but the storm took care of any evidence, if there had been any to begin with. I wish I had better news for you," Sheriff Raymond said.

"Thanks for looking," Paige said, sounding and feeling very disappointed.

Paige didn't intend to give up, not yet, not ever, not until she found the urn!

Garrett had been working from morning until night for four days since the Halloween dance. He caught a glimpse of himself in the mirror. He had dark sweat stains under his armpits, around his neck, and down the center of his shirt. His face looked dirty with whiskers of a beard and mustache. His body ached. Every muscle was sore, which no amount of liniment helped. He hoped that if he kept busy he wouldn't think about Paige, but he was wrong. Dead wrong. She filled his every thought.

He hadn't seen her since the seance. Garrett sighed. He had acted like an idiot that night. He should have kept his mouth shut, his temper under control. Now very few people in town would talk to him.

Times had changed in Patterson. The influence of the Taylors had dipped, while respect for the McCormicks had grown, probably because of the work Granny had done at the museum, and perhaps, her moonshine. People in town raved about how good and potent it was. Heck it must be, for Sheriff Raymond and Deputy Dave to look the other way.

Garrett brushed the dust from his jeans. He was a sight for sore eyes. Thank God no one would see him today. That thought had no more entered his head when the door bell rang. Well, at least the door bell worked. One of the few things that managed to function in this house. . . .

A frown drew his brows together as he descended the stairs to the first floor and made his way through the house. Who could this be? He wasn't expecting anyone. Could it be Paige? How he missed her. Four days without seeing her seemed more like four years. He longed to smell her perfume and gaze into her eyes. Most of all he missed talking with her, being with her.

He whipped the door open. A lightbulb flashed in his eyes. Garrett squinted and turned his attention to the woman standing next to the photographer.

She was dressed in a business suit, holding a pen and pad. "Are you Garrett Taylor, owner of the Taylor mansion?" she asked.

"Yes."

"I'm Cynthia Mattson, a freelance reporter from the Portland area, and this is my photographer, Kyle. I'd like to do a story on your haunted mansion. May we come in?"

At first Garrett couldn't find his voice. His mouth gaped open until he recovered saying, "Look, I'm very busy. So if you'll excuse me—"

Garrett took a step back and started to shut the door, but Kyle stuck his foot out, preventing the door from closing. Garrett clenched his fists, his temper aroused. He jerked the door open.

"Mr. Taylor," Cynthia pleaded, "we will only take a few minutes of your time."

"Did you ever think of calling first?" Garrett asked. "I could have saved you the trip and told you 'no' over the phone."

"Mr. Taylor, I think this is an interesting story, one the public would be interested in."

"Who put you up to this?"

"I don't understand," Cynthia said.

"Who called you about the Taylor mansion being haunted?"

"We don't reveal our sources. Please, Mr. Taylor."

"So it was someone from this town," Garrett said.

"What are you trying to hide?" Cynthia asked.

"Nothing. I need to get back to work." Garrett kicked the photographer's foot out of the way and slammed the door shut. "This is unbelievable," he muttered.

He didn't need a reporter to tell him who was behind this stunt. Dear, old Granny. He sighed in frustration, then rubbed his face. The woman pushed him too far. First the ghost, then the seance, and now this. What next?

Nothing! Because he'd see to it.

Garrett charged through the house and out a back door. Each step he took seemed to fuel his temper. Why couldn't she mind her own business? She had caused him nothing but trouble from the first day he had returned to Patterson. She thought she could win by pulling all these stunts, but she was wrong. Granny's actions motivated him to sell the mansion all the more.

He reached her apartment door and knocked. No one answered immediately so he pounded harder. Still no response. He turned the doorknob, finding it unlocked. Cracking the door he asked, "Anyone here?"

Nudging the door wide, he entered and treaded to the closed bathroom door. "Hello? Anyone here?" He tapped lightly.

Silence.

Garrett knew there was only one other place both Granny and Paige would be. He pivoted and surveyed the cracker box-sized room. A book on Granny's nightstand caught his eye. He moved closer. Picking up the book, he read the title aloud, *"Haunted Mansions in America."*

Chapter Seven

Garrett scanned the stack of books lying on the floor next to the bed. They all had to do with ghosts, haunted places, and the paranormal.

If the books weren't enough evidence that Granny was behind all of this, then he didn't know what would be.

"What are you doing in here?" Paige asked, standing in the doorway.

Garrett whirled around, still holding the book in his hands. He ignored her question and said, "I told you your grandmother was behind this ghost stuff."

Paige drew her perfectly shaped eyebrows together. "What are you talking about?"

"This." Garrett raised the book in the air. "Your grandmother has half a dozen books on haunted houses and ghosts. Look at them." He gestured to the pile on the floor.

Paige folded her arms over her chest, her eyes narrowing

to a glare. "So? Just because she has books on the subject doesn't mean she's haunting the mansion."

"What more do you need?" Garrett tossed the book on the bed and took several steps closer to Paige. He could smell her seductive perfume, and for a brief second he forgot what he was there for.

"I need a lot more evidence than that," Paige said.

"I don't. These books tell me quite clearly who's playing the piano and making noises in the house. Oh, and I really appreciate her sending that reporter over. I suppose your grandmother told them I'd agree to her writing an article about the ghost of the Taylor mansion. I'd really sell the place then, wouldn't I?"

"Granny didn't call anyone." Paige gripped the door-knob, her knuckles turning white. "In the words that you like to use so often—I'm going to have to ask you to leave."

Garrett strode over to her, standing so close she had to tilt her head back to meet his glare. In a low, threatening tone he said, "If I can prove your grandmother is behind the haunting, then I'll cancel the lease agreement. Null and void!"

He fisted his hands at his side, resisting the over-whelming urge to pull her into him and kiss her until her muscles went weak, until her knees buckled, and until she returned his passion.

Angered by his weakness for Paige, Garrett stormed by her and out the door, not looking back.

Ten days had passed since Paige had had her run-in with Garrett, yet she couldn't forget about it. Paige climbed in the shower, deep in thought. Could Garrett be right about

Granny haunting the mansion? She hoped he hadn't read the doubt in her eyes. Granny had told her that she had gotten the books from the library so she could be more informed about the situation. Her reasoning sounded plausible.

When Paige had seen Garrett in Granny's room, her heart leaped. She thought he had come to see her, but he hadn't. A part of her sympathized with Garrett. Selling the mansion was his choice, and his right, no matter who it might hurt. The seance did seem like a setup. Everyone at the table stared at him with accusing eyes as if he had murdered someone. Anyone would have become defensive.

Before Paige had come here, she could only see Granny's side of the situation. Since she had met Garrett and gotten to know him, she could definitely see there were two sides to every coin. She just wished he would be more open with her and tell her the real reason why he wanted to sell the mansion. She didn't buy his excuse of the expense and upkeep. No. Not with the millions he had inherited. Especially when she considered how much Rocky meant to Garrett. There was something more, something deeper that was pushing him to sell it. But what?

And how does the urn fit into all of this? Paige suspected the haunting and urn were connected because they had two things in common—the mansion and the time element, as both mysteries started at the same time.

During the last few days, she had asked around town about the robbery, but had come up with the same thing the sheriff had, nothing. No one had seen or heard anything. Which indicated to Paige that the burglar knew that on Sunday, Patterson was a virtual ghost town, and possibly that Granny was going to be visiting her sister that day.

Did that mean the burglar was a local? Or that the burglar was one of Granny's friends?

Garrett was convinced Granny was behind the hauntings. Paige was just as certain Granny had nothing to do with the robbery.

Paige searched her mind. She couldn't imagine Booker, Lily, Vivian, or Jean stealing anything. What would be their motive? Granny was the only one who had something to lose, unless Granny's friends were trying to help her. And where were Jean and Vivian during the seance? Could they have started the player piano? Could they have snuck out without anyone seeing them? The only other exits to the room were the windows. Both ladies were too arthritic to be climbing in and out of those.

Maybe Garrett was right, and the player piano just malfunctioned.

Paige finished showering, got dressed and hurried out the door to help Granny with another long, boring day at the museum. The place had such little business she was sure an abandoned cemetery would have had more visitors.

As she neared the door to the museum, she saw a line of people waiting to get in. What was going on? Paige hurried inside. Jean sat at the front desk selling tickets.

"Where's Granny?" Paige asked.

Jean pointed, too busy counting money to answer verbally.

Paige hurried over to the gift shop where Granny was filling the bookshelves in between selling merchandise. "Granny, what's happening? Why are all these people here?"

"They read the newspaper article about the mansion. I heard it was in a bunch of newspapers, not just Portland's, and was even featured on a television news report."

"What article?" Paige asked.

"The one the reporter wrote. She came around here about a week ago." Granny paused to look at Paige.

"Did she come in here and ask you questions?"

A wide smile spread on Granny's withered lips. "Had to. That Taylor boy wouldn't tell her anything. He practically threw her off the property." Granny pointed to the cash register. "Could you help me out here so I can get these books on the shelf?"

"Sure." Paige stood there for a moment watching Granny. She'd never seen her grandmother happier, smiling from ear to ear. She looked years younger with the stress from the past weeks having evaporated away.

A string of people stood in line to buy various items that the museum sold in their gift shop. Everything from books to postcards, and small craft items the ladies auxiliary donated to help the museum out. A book about the mansion and one about the history of the town, written and bound in binders by Granny, seemed to be the hot sellers. Years ago, Paige took all the photographs for the books when the mansion had been in its prime. Rocky and Gretta had wholeheartedly supported the project, letting Paige take a number of outside pictures of the mansion and its grounds.

Glancing around the museum, Paige's hope soared. She couldn't help it. With this kind of business, the museum would surely turn a profit, which meant that Granny and the museum could remain at the mansion. Garrett's words came crashing back into Paige's thoughts. If Granny was behind the haunting, then the deal was null and void. Paige prayed that wouldn't come to pass.

"Have you seen the ghost?" a woman asked, buying a book.

"No," Paige said, "but I have heard the music play by itself."

The woman gasped with delight, and her eyes widened. "Oh, I hope I can hear it. Does it usually play at night?"

Paige thought for a few seconds. "You know, come to think of it, most of the time the piano has played in the evening." She wondered if that was a clue and decided to store that information away for later.

"I plan to stand outside and listen for it tonight," the woman said.

Paige glanced at the sun streaming through the windows. "I think it will be a good night for that. Cold, but good." She bagged the book and handed it to the woman along with her change.

The woman smiled, then wandered back to the museum exhibits.

The place was packed. It had more customers in it today than it had since it had opened.

The day flew by quickly. Business didn't slow down until closing time. Everyone left except Paige and Granny, who had stayed behind to restock the gift store. The tourists had nearly cleaned the shop out.

Granny whistled while they worked.

The clanking of doors bursting open directed their attention to the entrance. Paige immediately spotted Garrett charging for them, then she glanced at Granny. A wide smile broke out on Granny's face as she stood and tugged the wrinkles out of her T-shirt that had a caricature of a ghost, and the words underneath, "Taylor Mansion. Patterson, Oregon." Vivian had hand painted several shirts, giving one to Granny and selling the rest.

Before Garrett could say a word, Granny said, "Like my

shirt? They're selling like hotcakes. You'd better get one before they're all gone." A cackle followed.

"Listen," Garrett said, his voice low, with a definite warning tone to it. "I don't want your lousy shirt, just like I don't want those tourists trespassing on my property. All day long they pounded on my doors, peeked in the windows, and trampled my new landscaping."

Granny raised her brows and shoulders. "Don't matter to me what they do or don't do."

Garrett's nostrils flared, and hands clenched at his side. Red showed through his tanned face.

Granny took no warning and continued. "I'd say we made a pretty damn good profit today. What we made today alone would turn a profit for the museum for the month. Looks like you lose."

"You called that reporter and convinced her to come here, didn't you?" Garrett demanded.

Granny stood her ground, her hands settling on her hips. "I did no such thing."

Garrett moved closer to Granny, and Granny matched him step for step until their bodies and faces were inches apart. Garrett's stare bore down on Granny, and Granny glared back, showing no fear.

Paige hurried over and forced herself between them, pushing them apart. "Calm down, both of you." She turned to Garrett first. "*We* can't do anything to keep those tourists off your property. You're going to have to call the sheriff and ask for his assistance." Then she turned to Granny. "And Granny, it's obvious Garrett is upset right now."

"Why are you taking his side?" Granny asked.

"She's not taking my side," Garrett shot back. "She's taking your side." He snorted. "The last thing your granddaughter would do is defend me. She won't even talk to me anymore, thanks to you."

Granny raised her bony fists, ready to duke it out with Garrett. "Well, do you blame her?"

Garrett pushed out a breath. "What are you doing? I'm not going to fight you."

"Chicken?"

"No, I'm not chicken. I'm not stupid either. I could knock you senseless with one punch, but since you're already there, what's the point?"

"Why you . . ." Granny leaned forward, swinging punches in the air.

Paige held her back. "Calm down!" Granny settled back on her heels, dropping her fists to her side. Paige glanced between them, exasperated at their behavior. "Look, you two. A lot has happened in a short time. All our nerves are frayed. We're tired, and we don't mean what we say."

"I do," Granny said.

"So do I," Garrett added.

Paige sighed, briefly closing her eyes. A whiff of Garrett's aftershave infiltrated her senses, making her knees weak. She cursed her attraction for him. Pushing that thought from her mind, she dealt with the matter at hand. "We can work this out."

"No, we can't," Granny said, folding her arms over her chest with a humph. "I had nothing to do with that reporter coming here."

"I don't believe you. You're the only one who has a reason to want this phony ghost story plastered in every newspaper in Oregon. You knew it would bring in curious tourists. You schemed up this whole ghost story to keep anyone from buying the mansion," Garrett said.

Granny grunted and flicked her hand as if waving off a pesky fly, her face contorted in a wrinkled sneer.

"Then tell me why are you reading paranormal books?" Garrett crossed his arms over his broad chest, the bicep muscles flexing with every movement.

Granny squinted, her glare fixed on him.

"Yeah, you didn't know I knew that, did you?" Garrett said.

Granny glanced at Paige for an explanation.

"I never told him," Paige said. "I found him snooping in our room the other day."

Granny's head jerked back to Garrett. "You have no right barging into my apartment and nosing around."

"No right? Have you forgotten I own this mansion?"

"I sure hope the new owner's more honorable. Your grandfather would be ashamed of you."

Garrett's head tilted back as if her words struck him in the face. He jabbed his finger in the air at her. "If I find out that you had anything to do with any of this ghost scheme, then plan on packing your bags, because our deal will be off, and you'll be out—you, and all of this." He swept his arms wide to indicate the contents of the museum.

"Garrett, please," Paige said.

He looked at her and his eyes were filled with sadness, or was it regret, or longing? "I'm sorry, Paige." Turning on his heels, he strode out of the museum.

The next day Vivian and Lily helped at the museum. Paige wanted Granny to take a break, but she had refused, saying this booming business came along once in a lifetime, and she wanted to enjoy every minute of it.

All night Paige tried to think of a way to resolve this dilemma, and finally she came up with a solution, that is, if Garrett would go for it. She got up early, primped, and dressed in a blue pant suit, then headed for the front of the mansion.

Taking a deep breath, Paige climbed the porch steps and knocked on the front door. When no one answered, she rang the doorbell. She waited and waited. Darn it. She really wanted to talk to Garrett, now, while she had her courage built up.

Just as she started to leave, the front door squeaked open.

"Paige," Garrett said. "I was wondering when you'd come."

The second her eyes met his face, she held her breath. He stood there clean-shaven, wearing a short-sleeved yellow shirt and jeans. His hair was neatly groomed, and his deep blue eyes reminded her of the color of a bluejay's feathers.

"I—uh—you were expecting me?" Paige asked.

"Yeah. You're looking for Buster, aren't you? He followed me in here this morning. It seems he's made himself at home in the parlor."

"I hope he hasn't been a bother," Paige said, retracing her steps to the door.

"No bother at all. I like him coming here. It gives me a chance to see you."

She tried to smile, but failed. "That's not why I came."

"Oh?" He raised his brows.

Paige fidgeted with her charm bracelet.

Garrett's gaze dipped to her hands, then returned to her face, but said nothing. He opened the door and gestured for her to come in.

Paige strolled inside and entered the parlor. Buster was

sprawled out on the sofa in deep sleep. "I hope he didn't break anything. I already owe you for a vase and figurine."

Garrett waved her comment away. "Don't worry about it. I have no use for such things." He stood in a wide stance several feet away, his arms crossed over his chest. He looked as if he were preparing for an attack. Did he think she came here to fight?

"So tell me, what brings you here?" he asked.

Paige clasped her hands together, then took a deep breath. Her heart pounded in her chest. She expected a negative response from Garrett, but how negative she wasn't sure. "I have a proposition for you." She hesitated a glance at him, and could tell she definitely had his attention.

"Please, continue," he said.

"I think I have a solution to our problem."

"Our problem? I think your grandmother is the only one with the problem."

Paige ignored his comment. "I would like to buy the mansion." She blurted it out as if it were a confession.

Garrett rubbed his chin, and stared at her.

Paige hastened on before he could say no. "I figured I could get a loan for one hundred thousand dollars. My savings would cover the down payment. I could give it to you in cash."

"One hundred thousand dollars. Do you have any idea what this house is worth?" His voice was calm.

"I know it's worth a lot more, but you don't want it and Granny does." She expelled the breath she had been holding. "It's all I have."

"I don't think so, Paige." He walked over to her until their bodies nearly touched. His finger ran along her cheek, stopping at her chin. His voice turned husky. "I think you have a lot more to offer than that."

Nervously, Paige licked her lips again. She raised her hands to his chest, then just rested them there. "Look, you want to get rid of this house, and Granny wants to keep it. This is a perfect solution."

"No."

"Why?" she asked.

"Because it's a matter of principle now. If your grandmother ends up with the mansion, then she'll think her scheme worked."

"So what?" Paige asked.

"It matters to me," Garrett said. "It's one thing to sell the mansion because it's a business deal. But it's another to be scared or scammed into selling it."

She shook her head. "Granny is not scamming you."

"Prove it," Garrett said.

Paige sighed in frustration. "I can't."

"Then, I'm sorry, but I can't sell you the mansion."

Despite the fire warming the room, the sudden tension erected a cool distance between them. In a very formal tone she said, "I'm sorry to have disturbed you." She quietly exited the house.

Garrett remained fixed to the rug.

When the door quietly clicked shut, he felt a sense of loneliness. Dammit. Why couldn't he get Paige McCormick out of his mind, out of his blood? One look was all it took to wanting to hold her in his arms and feel his lips upon hers. Day and night, all he thought about was her. Even in his dreams he couldn't escape, seeing her angelic face.

He wanted to sell her the mansion. Heck, wanted to give her the mansion. But he had his pride and refused to be bullied into a deal that wasn't best for him or his mother.

No. Not even the beautiful Paige McCormick could bewitch him into selling—or, more accurately—giving the house away.

The following day, Paige waited and watched for Garrett to leave the mansion. One way or another she would prove Granny's innocence—or guilt. Granny swore she had nothing to do with the haunting, and usually Granny didn't lie. But too much was at stake now. The mansion was her home, and the museum was her life, the thing that kept her going. Not only did running the museum give Granny a purpose, but the history of the town meant everything to her.

Paige wasn't sure what she would do if she found evidence that Granny was the ghost. Except that she knew she wouldn't tell Garrett.

At long last, Garrett left in his truck. Wasting no time, she sprinted across the front of the mansion. A curtain fluttering in a second-story bedroom—the grandparents' bedroom—caught her eye. She halted and narrowed her stare. The shut window indicated the wind hadn't blown the curtain, which meant someone was up there. Could it be Granny?

After finding the front door locked, Paige hurried around to the back of the house. Several times in the last few weeks she'd seen Garrett come and go through the back door, and noticed he had never locked it. The door opened with ease, despite the hinges creaking in protest from old age. She stepped into a dark hallway, her sneakers squeaking on the hardwood floor.

Footsteps sounded just above her head. Paige darted a look at the ceiling. Who could that possibly be? She knew it wasn't Garrett because she had just seen him leave. Instinct told her she was finally alone in the house with the person behind the haunting.

Trying to be as quiet as possible, she tiptoed to the bottom of the stairs. When she paused to listen, an eerie hush filled the house. The person upstairs was either hiding, or had somehow slipped out.

Paige wondered how far this person would go to keep his or her identity a secret. Could she be in danger? And what if this person wasn't Granny? Then why were ghosts appearing, unless . . . the house really was haunted?

Determination pushed her on. She had to know the truth. The entire situation filled her thoughts throughout the day— that, and Garrett's kisses.

She sighed. She would probably wonder her entire life about Garrett, what might have been between them. Pushing him away seemed to be the only thing she could do, given the circumstances. Unfortunately that didn't dull her desire for him. Every time she was in the same room with him, her body would react, crying out for his gentle touch, his tender caresses.

Paige reached the top stair and carefully made her way down the hall to the master bedroom. As if oxygen would strengthen her courage, she sucked in a breath before she entered.

No one was there, at least in plain sight. She checked the bathroom, then opened the closet's double doors. A musty odor greeted her. The closet was deep and long; it was the biggest closet she'd ever seen. "A person could live in here," Paige muttered to herself.

Rows of clothes hung on rods, and shoe boxes were stacked on the floor. Paige opened one of the boxes closest to her; inside was a black pair of shoes. On a rod near the back of the closet, Paige noticed all the clothes had been pushed to one side.

She stepped further inside and searched for a light switch, feeling along the wall. Finding one, she flipped it on, but the bulb was dead. No sense exploring when she couldn't see. Turning abruptly, Paige kicked something hard. *Ouch,* that had hurt. She squinted down, peering at what felt as hard and heavy as a boulder.

Her eyes widened.

She gasped!

Chapter Eight

P aige crouched down and ran her fingers over the cold smooth metal, then nudged it into the light. She felt like crying with relief as she stared at the urn. The one symbol of honor in her family, and she found it. Now it could go back to the museum where it belonged. All would again see that, for one shining moment in history, a McCormick stood above the rest.

Paige lifted the urn, her muscles straining from its weight. She carried it to the bed and sat down, placing it beside her. What was the urn doing in Garrett's house? She felt anger tighten her stomach into a knot. Could Garrett have stolen it? No. Impossible. He had rescued her from the runaway balloon only minutes later. Of course, she drifted for a while between the time she had spotted the thief and the time Garrett had come to her rescue. But would that have given him enough time to hide the urn and then save her?

She lifted it again, gauging how heavy it was. Granny couldn't have taken it. She couldn't have carried it ten feet. Besides, what would her motive be? The insurance money? No. Many things were more important to Granny than money, especially the urn.

Paige looked around the room. This was Garrett's house. He had been the only one working here for weeks. Plus, at night, he locked the place up tighter than a sealed drum. Garrett had to be the thief, or he had someone do the stealing for him, like his dear, sweet cousin who just happened to deal in antiques.

But why? Maybe he thought it was the only way to get Granny and the museum out of his mansion for good.

So why was she sitting here when she could go ask him? Returning the urn to the closet for safekeeping, Paige hurried through the house and out the front door. As she crossed the mansion grounds in the direction of town, her anger mounted. How many times had Garrett accused her family of being dishonest? Even recently he'd blamed Granny for haunting the house. And look who had the evidence stashed away in the closet.

On Main Street, Paige spotted Garrett's truck, parked in front of the hardware store. She couldn't wait until she got her hands on him. He'd better have a good excuse, or she would . . . well, she wasn't sure what she'd do, but she'd do something.

She peered inside the hardware store's front window. A couple of dairy farmers were chatting with Garrett.

Paige burst through the door and charged up to Garrett. He looked surprised to see her, and a bit confused.

"Are you looking for me?" Garrett asked.

"Darn right I am."

Garrett frowned, then glanced at the men he had been talking with. "Excuse me," Garrett said. As Garrett turned to face her, the men walked away, but kept within hearing distance.

Before Garrett could get a word out, Paige said, "How dare you?"

"What's going on?"

"How dare you throw accusations at my grandmother when all along you had the urn? And you call my family dishonest! I think you'd better take a long look in the mirror, buddy."

Garrett's brows drew together. "Am I supposed to know what you're talking about?"

Paige shook her head in disgust. "Can't you at least own up to it? You got caught; okay. Now you have to pay the piper."

Garrett glanced around the store.

Paige knew everyone was watching, but she didn't care. Garrett Taylor deserved a little humiliation, especially after what he had put her family through.

Clutching her arm, he dragged her outside, shutting the door behind her with a firm click. "Now would you please tell me what this is all about?"

Paige jerked her arm free. "As if you don't know. Okay, I'll humor you. I found the urn in your grandparents' closet. Tell me, what was it doing in there?"

"Maybe you should tell me what you were doing in my house uninvited."

"You're changing the subject," Paige said.

"And I think you've gotten into your grandmother's moonshine. I don't have your urn. I just worked in my grandparents' room yesterday. I never saw the urn. Are you sure it's there?"

"Yes, I'm sure." Paige spat the words out.

Simultaneously, they glanced through the hardware store window. Everyone had their ears and faces pressed against the glass trying to listen in. They made no attempt to hide their curiosity.

Garrett lowered his voice. "I think we'd better go check this out." His fingers wound around her arm again. This time, he was much more gentle. After they crossed the street, he dropped his hand to his side. They walked at a brisk pace back to the mansion.

Paige wished he hadn't touched her. Because the moment he had, she felt a warmth spread through her. Why couldn't her anger insulate her from him? She wanted that. She hated her attraction to him, and that Jell-O feeling that came over her whenever he was near.

Garrett unlocked the front door and led the way through the foyer. He jumped three stairs at a time, reaching the bedroom first. He charged straight to the closet and peeked in. "Where is it?"

"It's right there," Paige said breathlessly, coming up behind him. She pushed past him and searched the closet. "I put it right here," she said, jabbing her finger at the floor where she had set it.

The urn was gone. Disappeared. Vanished into thin air. "I swear I put it right here." She shot him an accusing glare. "What did you do with it? Where is it?"

Garrett drew his brows together. "Are you feeling all right?"

Paige tightened her hands into balls. She could feel the heat rushing to her face, and her throat tighten. "I swear to you, I left the urn sitting right here on the floor of this closet!"

Garrett hesitated, then said, "I believe you. I think some-one's playing games with us. And I can guess who it is."

"You're wrong. The urn was heavier than lead. I strug-gled with it. There's no way Granny could have carried it, not with her arthritis."

"Paige," he said as if his patience were being tested, "putting the urn in the Taylor mansion would be something Granny would do to get back at me. I really lost my temper the other day. I admit I was a jerk."

"And wrong." She smiled.

"I wouldn't blame Granny if she tried to get back at me."

"But Granny wouldn't do this, Garrett. Don't you un-derstand? The urn means way too much to her. She wouldn't have stolen it. She can't even talk about it without getting choked up."

Garrett sighed, then ran his fingers through his hair while he paced across the room. He pivoted and said, "Then who? Why?"

Paige shrugged. "I wish I knew." So many questions were unanswered. She needed to find the answers, and soon. Time was running out.

"I have to get back to the hardware store," Garrett said. "I've got a load of supplies to pay for."

"I'd like to stay and look around if you don't mind."

"Not at all." Garrett hesitated before he added, "I'm re-ally sorry about losing my temper with your grandmother. That's not like me at all."

Paige smiled. "Granny has a tendency to bring out the worst in people."

Garrett chuckled with a nod.

As soon as he disappeared from sight, Paige returned to the closet. She would turn the place inside out if she had to. First, she started by opening every box, but found only shoes. Next, she combed through the drawers and shelves. Nothing. No hint of who might be playing games with them, and no hint of the urn.

Buster wandered into the closet, meowed, then rubbed his head and body against Paige's leg.

"Hi Buster," she said. "How's my pretty kitty?" She crouched down to pet him, rubbing the sides of his neck.

Buster purred his appreciation. Satisfied, he continued further into the closet, disappearing under a rack of clothes.

Paige returned to the bedroom and searched for a flashlight, finding one in a nightstand. She flicked it on and was surprised when the light shined bright, as if new batteries had recently been put in. . . .

Paige reentered the closet and beamed the light on the thick row of clothes. A variety of styles hung on the rack: fancy dresses, casual slacks, silk blouses, and nightgowns. Apparently, Rocky couldn't part with his wife's belongings after her death. That didn't surprise Paige. Granny had the same problem of letting go. She still had her husband's stuff stored in boxes. Heck, she still had grandpa in the urn!

"Don't get into anything, Buster," Paige said. "I already owe Garrett for the things you've broken. I'll be penniless by the time we leave Patterson if you keep coming in the mansion."

The closet became quiet, too quiet. Normally when she talked to Buster he would purr, or meow, or be into something. "Buster. Where'd you go? Here, kitty, kitty."

Paige slid the clothes to one side, and flashed the light on the floor in an area behind the rack. A horizontal gap at the base of the floor caught her attention. She followed it with the light. It was a door. What was a door doing inside a closet?

She ducked under the rack. The door was cracked open, just wide enough for an agile cat to get through. When she pushed the door wide, it made no sound; the hinges must have been freshly lubricated. A dark, long and narrow stairway appeared before her. Cobwebs stretched from the ceiling to the walls.

"Buster," she called. "Come here, kitty."

Carefully, she made her way up the stairs, and was surprised the steps were sturdy and made little noise. When she was nearly to the top stair her foot came down on something hard. Paige grabbed the railing to keep her balance, while mumbling a few expletives.

"Is this one of your toys, Buster, or another broken item I'm going to have to pay for?"

She picked up the object, placed it in her pocket, and continued on. At the top of the stairs was another door, also ajar. It, too, made no sound when she nudged it open.

The music room appeared before her.

Paige realized the significance of this find. A hidden passageway allowed a person easy access to the room and player piano without being seen. She walked over to the main entrance of the music room and turned.

Why hadn't she seen this door before? She surveyed the room, noticing the door had been designed to blend in with the wall. Did Garrett know about this secret passageway?

Buster jumped onto the bench in front of the player piano. He sniffed at the keys and looked bored when he discovered it wasn't something he could play with or eat.

"So, what do I owe Garrett for now?" Paige asked as she remembered the smooth object in her pocket.

She examined it carefully—it resembled a television remote control. This was definitely not Buster's toy, or something a cat could have carried. No. A person had to have dropped it.

What could the remote belong to? Curious, she pressed the small round buttons. Suddenly, the player piano roared into song.

Frightened, Buster leaped off the bench and scampered out of the room, down the main stairs.

Paige gasped, quickly pressing all the buttons. Just as abruptly as the music began, the player piano shut off.

A deafening quiet followed.

The implication of this clue was clear. Now the big questions remained. Who was doing this? And why?

Lester Bradford returned three weeks to the day of his first visit. When he entered the mansion, Garrett could tell Lester was impressed with the progress. The place did look considerably better. No more cobwebs, no more sheets, no more layers of dust. The hardwood floors shined, the banister was polished to a glossy finish, and fires burned in many of the fireplaces, giving the mansion a warm, homey feeling. A scent of apple pie filled the room, an old trick Garrett had learned from a realtor.

Lester said nothing as he wandered from room to room, only nodding his head. Finally he stopped at the base of the stairs. "I can't believe this is the same place. I hardly recognized it from the outside. And I definitely don't recognize the inside."

Garrett felt proud. His hard work showed. He had to admit the place had started to grow on him. But he had no choice. Selling the mansion was his only option. Like it or not.

"You've put so much work into the house I almost hate

to tell you that I've decided to tear it down and rebuild, retaining the Taylor name, of course," Lester said.

Garrett's chest tightened as if the wind had been knocked out of him. "You intend to tear it down? Why?"

"Because it's more cost effective. The house is old. Needs new plumbing and wiring. The foundation is good, though. So I'll keep it along with a few other things. But other than that, the rest of the place goes."

Garrett's body numbed. "What about the agreement with the museum and Granny McCormick?"

"That's the beauty of this. If I tear it down and rebuild, there will be no agreement, and I can get that eccentric woman out of my hair." Lester grinned. "Tearing the mansion down will clear out all the ghosts too." He chuckled.

Garrett's defenses rose. "Granny's not eccentric. She just loves this mansion and the museum."

Lester shrugged as if he didn't really care either way. "I'll leave you with my offer. Look it over carefully. I'm sure you'll find it more than generous."

He handed Garrett a thick envelope. "As soon as this is signed, I'm having an architect come out to design a large hotel with an attached shopping mall, an indoor pool, and other amenities for guests to come, stay, and relax."

"A shopping mall in Patterson?" Garrett said.

"Yes. It's about time someone updated this town. And who better to do it than me?" Lester strolled to the front door, rested his hand on the knob, and turned to address Garrett, who had halted several feet away. "By the way, I might have to move that cemetery."

"Lester, that cemetery has been here for centuries. It's a historical landmark. You can't just move it."

Lester smiled. "Just watch me." With a wave, he was out the door.

Garrett plodded to the door and watched as Lester's Lexus disappeared out of sight. A sick heavy knot rested in the pit of Garrett's stomach. Tear the mansion down? Build shops and a swimming pool? Move the cemetery?

Now he felt utterly disloyal to his grandfather. What kind of grandson was he to sell this place after everything his grandfather had done for him?

"I heard what the developer said," Anne said, walking out of the dining room and over to him.

Garrett whipped around. "You startled me."

Her saddened eyes spoke louder than words.

"How much did you hear?" Garrett asked.

"All of it." She sighed. "Your grandfather loved this place. And he loved you too, Garrett. He trusted you to take care of his home, live in it, raise a family here."

"I don't want to get into this with you again. We hashed this out over the phone before I came back."

"And we're going to talk about it again. Right here. Right now." She went over to Garrett, placed her hands on his shoulders, and looked him straight in the eye. "I know you're selling this place in an effort to protect me, protect our past. But I'm telling you, son, there's nothing to protect. Yes, your father neglected you. And if your grandparents hadn't stepped in, social services would have removed you from our home."

Garrett distanced himself from her, stepping into the parlor, and stopping at the fireplace. He rested his hands on the mantle, and gazed at the photographs of his grandparents, of his parents, and of himself. He didn't want to hear this, he didn't want to relive the pain of those years, the embarrassment, the constant fear of someone finding out, and the need to hide it from everyone, even God, if he could have.

He sensed her presence behind him, but he made no effort to turn around.

"Garrett how is selling this place going to heal the past? It's not. You're running away."

He dropped his head forward. "Mother," he said with pain in his voice, pain in his heart. "You and father left me alone for days, sometimes weeks. It was always business. Neither one of you ever had time for me. We had to move in with Grandma and Grandpa because you weren't able to take care of me." He sighed. He didn't want to hurt her, or blame her, but that's exactly what it sounded like. "If I sell the mansion, then neither one of us has any reason to stay here. You could move to Portland with me and start a new life."

"And you think if we move away, then our secret will stay with us forever?"

He turned to face her. He couldn't recall a time while growing up when she had looked this good, this happy. "Yes," he replied.

"What about Paige?" Anne asked.

"She's not interested in me." He felt a pressure build in his chest from the lie.

"You're mistaken. She's more than interested in you. She's in love with you. And you with her. You two are both so stubborn, unwilling to yield even a little bit, you can't allow yourselves to see it."

"You're wrong."

"Am I? I saw the way you two looked at each other at the dance. I've been wrong about many things in my life, but not this."

Garrett quickly changed the subject. "Look, I know you love this place. I do too. But I've got to protect you."

"From what?" She crossed her arms over her chest.

"From gossip. From ridicule."

Anne laughed in disgust. "Garrett, the only one you're protecting is yourself. I love you. But you're an absolute fool if you think this entire town doesn't already know about our past."

Quiet loomed between them for many long seconds.

"I'll leave you alone to think about what I've said. But Garrett, you'd better do something to keep Paige here, or you'll be losing someone with whom you could have had a wonderful life. Stop punishing yourself for the past. You did nothing wrong. You deserve to be happy. I think you two could be very happy together. Considering the opposite economic backgrounds you and Paige came from, you both have a lot in common."

Garrett listened to her shoes click on the hardwood floor as she crossed the room, exiting out the front door. Silence filled the house, except for the crackling of the fire. He stared at the flames.

She was right. He was selling the house because of his own fears. His mother had obviously come to terms with the past, but he hadn't. Unfortunately, knowing that and accepting it were two different things.

There had been times when he had wanted to thrash his mother and father for never being there for him. Worse yet, his father had blamed Garrett for all his failures. Every business deal that went sour had been Garrett's fault.

Garrett vowed his whole life he would succeed where his father had failed. Goal one had been accomplished: He had the successful business. Goal two remained: having the happy family, a loving wife, and children to raise and nurture. He would give his family everything he never had, everything that truly mattered—love, praise, himself. He'd be there for his children's activities: he'd help them with schoolwork. He'd listen to their problems; he'd always be there to hear how their day went.

Growing up in Patterson had been lonely for him. Sure, he had friends from school, but they hardly replaced a parent's love and approval.

Funny how most people believed that making a lot of money equalled success in life. But Garret knew firsthand that what really mattered in life wasn't fame or fortune, but the love you gave and shared with others.

Garrett spent the next couple of days alone, sorting through his thoughts. He weighed the pros and cons of selling the mansion. Money wasn't an issue and never had been. He could retire on half of what his grandfather had left him.

His mother was right. He was running away, blaming himself for his past and his parents' past. Now he had to stop running. He had to let go of everything, his parents' problems, the past. By seeing his parents as human beings who made mistakes, who had their strengths and weaknesses, and who were hurting for reasons beyond his control, then he could ease the anger simmering inside him. Healing could only begin with forgiveness.

Now, seeing his situation from an adult perspective and not from the child's, he finally realized he had done nothing wrong. His father's problems were just that—his father's problems.

Garrett realized he had accomplished much in his life, and if his father didn't think it was good enough, then his father would have to deal with that, not him.

Healing this deep-seated wound would take time, but eventually he knew it would happen. But he didn't have as much time if he intended to keep Paige in his life. He needed her. With Paige, he could overcome anything. He couldn't lose her. He wouldn't lose her. So he formed a plan, one he hoped would work.

Garrett checked his watch. Paige should be here any minute. He opened a bottle of wine and set it in an ice bucket to let it chill. His heart beat a little faster when he heard her knock. Crossing the foyer, he whipped open the door.

Paige stood there wrapped in a thick warm coat, her cheeks rosy from the cold air. She never looked more beautiful to him than she did at this moment.

"I think it might snow tonight," Paige said as she entered the foyer, rubbing her hands together. She appeared to be reserved, unsure, and probably a bit curious.

"Let me take your coat," Garrett said, and hung it on a rack near the front door. He guided her into the parlor. "I—uh—I wanted to apologize for the other day. I spoke rather harshly to you." He dipped his head. Confessions were never one of his strengths, nor did he make them often.

Paige's face softened with concern. "I'm sorry too, Garrett." She hesitated before saying, "Is that why you asked me over tonight?"

"I didn't invite you over tonight just to apologize."

"Ulterior motives, huh?" she said in a teasing fashion, then smiled. She was doing it with him again, flirting.

Garrett couldn't suppress a grin. His emotions always seemed to be at such extremes with Paige, either elated or angry. Maybe in time he would find a middle ground. "I made us dinner. You hungry?" He motioned with his arm for her to lead the way into the room.

"No diner food today?"

"Nope. You're stuck with my cooking." Garrett followed

her into the dining room, then held the chair out, scooting it as she sat down. Instead of placing himself across the table from her, he sat adjacent to her. He could see the puzzled expression on her face, and knew she had good reason to be confused. The last time they spoke he had put distance between them. He hoped to narrow the gap.

He talked while he filled both their plates with seasoned steaks, baked potatoes, and steamed carrots and broccoli. "I was looking through books featuring your work last night. I particularly like the photographs you took in Ethiopia. They were very moving, very compelling."

She studied him for several long seconds. "Thank you. That's what I was after. A lot of people don't understand I'm trying to convey real-life emotions in my photographs. Sometimes a picture speaks louder than words."

"Yours definitely do. You're very talented."

Paige frowned. "I don't get it, Garrett. Yesterday you were upset with me. And now you're complimenting me on my work. I almost feel like you're flattering me because you want something."

"You don't trust anyone, do you?" He shook his head. "I don't want anything from you, Paige. I want to get to know you better. That's all."

"And nothing else?" She looked at him with suspicion in her eyes.

"No." He lifted his shoulders. "What are you thinking?"

"I'm thinking that you think I know something, but I don't know what you think I might know."

"Come again?" he asked.

"About the hauntings." She sounded exasperated.

Finally, it dawned on Garrett what she was talking about. "You're sure suspicious." He gazed into her eyes, leaned forward and said, "My intent is purely personal. Nothing more."

Her cheeks flushed slightly.

"Is it so hard to believe I'm attracted to you, and I enjoy being with you?"

Paige cast her eyes to her plate, and didn't offer a reply.

"Now that we've cleared that up," Garrett said, "would you like a roll?" He held the basket out to her.

Through the rest of the meal, they talked about happy times and funny incidents in their past, about their careers, and what the future might hold. The relaxed atmosphere, and probably the wine allowed them to talk freely.

After putting the dishes in the kitchen, they retired to the parlor. Garrett stoked the fire, and soon a blaze glowed in the room. He took a seat beside Paige on one of the sofas.

Paige removed her shoes and curled her feet up, then faced him. She looked comfortable and at ease. "You never told me what you wanted to talk to me about."

Garrett let his gaze drift from her eyes, down her petite nose, to her full lips. He loved the angles of her cheekbones and jaw, so clean, so pure. "I wanted to talk to you about you and me teaming up to find your family's urn."

Her eyes widened and she tilted her head. "Really?"

"Yes. I think when we find the urn, we'll find the culprit who's haunting the house."

"I agree."

"You agree with us teaming up together, or you agree that the person who stole the urn also is behind the hauntings?"

"Both."

"Good." His gaze dipped to her throat, so smooth and enticing. "But first we have some unfinished business . . . and I won't take 'no' for an answer."

Paige frowned.

Chapter Nine

Garrett moved closer. He couldn't resist any longer. With his lips inches from hers, he said, "I'm in love with you, Paige. I fell in love with you the day we met in the balloon." When his mouth claimed hers, she surrendered completely. Garrett had anticipated resistance, and when none came, that only heightened his wanting her all the more.

Paige met his urgent kisses with those of her own, drawing a groan from him. He slid his fingers into her long hair, the silky texture gliding easily through. He moved his hands to her back and pulled her to him, wanting her closer.

Lifting his mouth only inches from hers, he said, "I need you, Paige."

Paige closed her eyes, waiting for the panic to well inside, but it didn't come. Normally when a man started needing her, that's when she backed away, or ran. Why didn't she feel that way with Garrett? What made him so different?

"You are the most beautiful woman I've ever seen," Garrett whispered. "I don't want to ever let you go."

Again, Paige waited for the panic to grip her. Instead, she was filled with elation, an emotion that told her that this moment between them was right.

Paige felt like she had been a dry stick of dynamite, never having the right spark to awaken the depth of love she'd kept buried deep inside. She had known somewhere there was a person that would touch her heart, and draw out the love she had managed to hide so well. How could she have ever guessed it would be Garrett?

"I never knew I could love someone like this," Paige said. She gazed into the fire, hoping her pulse would soon return to normal.

"I didn't either," Garrett said. "Will you stay the night?"

"I still think we need to resolve our—problems—before we get more involved."

He took several long seconds to think about it. "Okay. But do stay. I've got a comfortable couch waiting for you." Being with her was enough for him for now.

Paige smiled and nodded.

Tonight Paige wouldn't fear a ghost appearing before them. She wouldn't fear many things anymore.

The next morning, Paige woke up to a warm fire, the smell of hotcakes cooking on the griddle, and coffee brewing. She followed the scent into the kitchen.

"Good morning," Garrett said as he flipped a large hotcake. He poured her a cup of coffee and handed it to her.

Paige took a sip, then met his gaze.

"You look gorgeous in the morning." He leaned forward,

placing a kiss on her lips. "Mmmm. Maybe I'll have you for breakfast instead."

Paige could feel her cheeks warm at the thought.

"Too bad we don't have time, partner," Garrett said.

"Partner?"

"We have a case to solve, remember? The mystery of the stolen urn."

"You mean the mystery of the stolen grandpa."

Garrett frowned. "What are you talking about?"

"The urn has my grandfather's ashes in it."

"You're kidding, right?"

"I wish I were. Granny was supposed to spread his ashes out by the lake." She smiled. "Grandpa always loved the woods. He said he felt one with nature when he was out in the forest, usually hunting." She met his stare. "Grandpa was a lousy shot. I think he went out hunting more to get away and be alone, than to shoot an animal for meat."

"So why are his ashes still in the urn?" Garrett slapped a couple of large hotcakes on a plate and handed them to Paige.

"Granny couldn't part with him. She said having his ashes made her feel like he was still around. Granny hasn't parted with anything of Grandpa's. She really loved him. They had a wonderful marriage, the kind that comes around once in a lifetime if you're lucky."

Garrett locked eyes with Paige. He didn't have to utter a word. She knew what he was thinking, that they too could have the same kind of relationship.

She took a bite of food so she wouldn't have to say anything.

He cleared his throat. "So where do we start? With the Sheriff, maybe?"

Paige shook her head, chewed, and swallowed. "No. I

didn't get anywhere with him. Besides, I also asked around town and no one saw or heard anything."

Garrett leaned on the counter and sipped his coffee. "Have you looked for clues in the museum?"

"No, Granny cleaned the mess up right after the Sheriff investigated. She didn't want a museum visitor to get cut by the broken glass."

"So who are our suspects?" He continued on. "Granny."

"Your cousin, what was her name?" Paige quickly added.

"Jeannie." A tension arose between them. "Look," Garrett said, "we can't become defensive about the suspects. We have to look at the situation with an objective eye. The minute emotions become involved, then our opinions get clouded."

"Agreed," Paige said.

A moment of silence filled the room while they contemplated who it could be. "Another possible suspect could be any one of your grandmother's friends," Garrett said.

"I've thought about that." Paige stared across the room, pondering. "Booker would be the most likely candidate."

"I would think Lily would," Garrett said. "She's the most knowledgeable about the paranormal."

Paige set her plate on the counter. "What does that have to do with the urn?"

"I thought we agreed that the house being haunted and the urn being stolen were connected," Garrett said.

She nodded. "I guess you're right. But that would make Booker an even more likely candidate. He'd be strong enough to steal the urn—"

"And he was the one who ran into the dance and announced the music was playing."

Paige's mind raced in many different directions. She suddenly changed the subject, saying, "Garrett, how well do you know this house?"

"What kind of question is that? I've been working on it for weeks. I lived here when I was young all the way through high school."

"So you know about the secret stairway?" She wanted to catch him off guard to get a genuine reaction.

He lifted his brows, and his mouth dipped. "I had forgotten about it. How'd you know?"

"I found it by accident, along with something else." She hesitated. Should she tell him about the remote?

"What?"

"Follow me," Paige said. She led the way back to her coat, snatched the remote from her pocket, then climbed the stairs with Garrett right behind her. When they reached the music room, she stopped at the door. Pressing the button, Paige turned to look at Garrett as the player piano started.

He looked at her, the remote, then back to her. "Where'd you find that?" He took it from her hands, and pressed a button shutting the music off.

"I stumbled on it when I went up the hidden stairway."

"Well I'll be dammed." Garrett studied the remote.

"Then you didn't know about this?" Paige asked.

His head turned sharply, and his brows drew together. "No. Are you kidding? If I'd known about this, I'd have been searching for it to prove to your grandmother and the entire town that this place wasn't haunted. I knew I was right."

"The remote explains the 'how', but not the 'who' or 'why,' let alone the missing urn."

"Then again, maybe it does," Garrett said. "Look." He turned over the remote. An old faded sticker was on the back. "Looks like this came from Booker's Fix-It Shop." He smiled at her. "I think we found our culprit."

"Booker." Paige said his name aloud hoping it would convince her that they indeed had their man, but it didn't work. Instinct told her they were wrong.

She shook her head.

"Why not?" Garrett asked.

"It doesn't make sense. Why would Booker haunt the house?"

He stared at her as if she was dense. "Because he wanted to help your grandmother. He thought ghosts in the mansion would scare the developer away."

"And what about the urn? Booker knew what the urn and Grandpa's ashes meant to Granny. He'd never steal it. What would he have to gain?"

"Maybe they're not connected." Garrett met her stare for several long seconds before he said, "We need to pay a visit to Booker."

After Paige and Garrett dressed, they walked down the street, heading for the opposite end of town where Booker had his part-time fix-it shop.

"Garrett, we can't just barge in there and accuse him of everything."

"I'll be diplomatic," Garrett said.

"I think I should do the talking." Paige lowered her voice. "You're not exactly on Booker's good list. He'll open up more to me than you."

Garrett reluctantly agreed, remembering the challenging look Booker gave him at the dance. At the time, Garrett thought Booker just didn't like the thought of Paige getting close to him because of Granny. Now Garrett wondered if there wasn't more to it, like Booker trying to hide his involvement with the hauntings and the urn.

A bell attached to the top of the door jingled when they entered. Booker's fix-it shop was small, cramped and cluttered. He had several projects half-done and sprawled out over the counter. Booker was nowhere in sight, but his pet pig, laying next to a small cast-iron woodstove, was snoring away.

"Hello, anyone here?" Paige asked.

"Give me a second," Booker said from the back room. Several minutes later, he appeared and stepped to the counter. His eyes lit up seeing Paige, then quickly darkened as his gaze drifted to Garrett.

"What brings you by?" Booker addressed Paige as if Garrett wasn't even in the room.

"Well," Paige began, "we found this in the Taylor mansion, and I was wondering if you know what it is and where it came from."

Booker took the remote in his hands and turned it over. "My, my. I haven't seen this thing in a few years. Does it still work?"

"Work on what?" Garrett asked.

"Why, I made this remote for your granddaddy to turn the player piano on and off. His arthritis got so bad in his last few years that he couldn't play the piano any longer. So he had me order this remote for him. I had to practically reconstruct the piano so a remote would work with it. Cost your grandpappy a couple grand to get it done." Booker shook his head. "I'd forgotten all about it."

"You sure about that?" Garrett said.

Booker's head jerked up, his eyes narrowing in on Garrett. "If you have something to say, just say it."

"Garrett doesn't mean anything by it," Paige said hastily.

"Yes, I do. I think you are haunting my house. And this remote proves it."

Booker placed his massive hands on the counter and leaned toward Garrett. "You tell me just how this proves anything." He glared at Garrett, daring him to speak.

Garrett refused to be intimidated by the man and moved closer until their faces were only inches apart. "The remote has your name on it. Plus, you were the one on Halloween night who announced to everyone at the dance about the music playing. Coincidence? I don't think so."

"Why I ought to throw you out of here." Booker's nostrils flared.

"Calm down, you two," Paige said in an uneasy voice. "Garrett didn't mean it the way it sounded. Booker, do you know anyone else who knew about the remote?"

Booker lifted his head, the tension easing from his forehead. "Garrett's mother knew about it."

"How about Granny?"

Booker thought, then shook his head. "Nope."

Paige's voice became quiet. "Booker, do you know anyone who would want to scare people away from the house?"

He shrugged. "No. Can't say as I do."

"What about the urn? Do you know anyone who might have stolen the urn?"

Rubbing his forehead, Booker said, "You know, I've thought about that a lot, and I can't think of a single reason why someone would steal that urn."

"Other than the value of the gold," Garrett said.

Booker squinted his eyes, returning his sneer back on Garrett. The quiet in the room almost crackled. His voice lowered. "Granny is one of my best friends. We go way back. I'd put myself in harm's way to get back that urn for her." A moment lingered before he added, "Does that answer all your questions?"

"Thanks, Booker. We appreciate your help," Paige said, then grabbed Garrett's arm, pulled him outside, and shut the door behind them.

"Well, you handled that real smoothly." Her sarcasm came across loud and clear.

"Sorry. The guy irritates me."

She forced a laugh. "And you irritate him."

They walked back toward the mansion in silence.

Halfway there, Garrett said, "Where do we go from here?"

Paige sighed. "Another dead end."

"Maybe."

She darted a sideways glance at him. "What do you mean?"

"Booker could be lying—"

"No. I would have known if he was lying. Booker can't look you in the eyes when he lies. I've seen it a dozen times when he's playing poker." They walked the rest of the way in quiet contemplation.

When they reached the porch, Garrett unlocked the front door. "I'm sure glad those tourists stopped coming around. I still get a few on the weekends, but that's it." He held the door open for Paige to enter.

She strolled into the parlor. "Garrett."

The nervousness in her voice caught his attention.

"What are you going to do when the time is up?" Paige asked.

"I'll ask you to marry me. Heck, I might even throw in the house just so you'll say yes." Garrett wasn't sure what made him say that. When had he become impulsive? But it sounded right, felt right.

Her lips wavered between a smile and a frown.

He could tell she didn't know whether to take him seriously or not. So he decided to answer that question for her. Reaching out, he nestled her into his arms. Without saying a word, he gave her a long, slow kiss. The instant their lips touched, Garrett wanted more. He marveled at her ability to ignite his hunger for her.

"Garrett," Paige whispered.

"Shhh," he said. "Not now." He knew she wanted to give him every reason under the sun why they couldn't be together. Frankly, he didn't want to hear them. Silencing any further argument, he kissed her again.

Garrett lifted her into his arms and carried her up the stairs, taking two at a time, and entered the master bedroom. He set her on the bed, then shut the curtains. When he tried to kick his shoes off and they wouldn't fall off, Paige laughed.

She tugged hers off and leaned over the side of the bed and let them drop.

Garrett hobbled over to the bed, struggling with one foot, and cursing because his laces were in a knot. He flopped down on the bed and worked on the knot.

"What's this?" Paige sat up and handed Garrett a business card. "I found it on the floor beside the bed."

Garrett looked at Lester's card, then shrugged. He must have dropped it when he was looking at the room."

"I was here with you," Paige said. "I don't remember seeing him drop anything. Plus, when I found the urn in here the other day, I sat down on this very spot and didn't see a card on the floor."

"Paige, you weren't looking for it. You were too absorbed in the urn."

"True. But I think I would have noticed it." She took the card from his hands and stared at the bright red embossing. "This could be a clue."

"A clue to what?" Garrett asked.

She tilted her head and looked at him as if he was denser than a log soaked in water. "Don't you see? If Lester Bradford didn't drop this when he was here with us, then that means he came back." Her excitement started to show. "And who would have more motive to haunt this place than the very man who wants to buy it?"

Garrett held his hands up. "Whoa. Slow down." He hesitated before he continued. "What you don't know is that Lester was here two days ago." He glanced away. A long pause followed, filled with a building tension.

At long last Paige said, "He was?"

Garrett looked back at her. "Yes."

"And?"

"And he made me an offer."

"Did you accept the offer?"

"Not yet."

"What are you going to do?" Paige asked.

"I'm not sure. I haven't read the contract."

She tilted her head. "For a man that can't wait to unload this place, I'd think the contract would have been your first priority."

His gaze drifted to the window. A tightening grew into a hard knot in the pit of his stomach. "I don't want to talk about it."

"You want me to be your wife, but you won't talk to me. I don't call that open communication between two people who love each other."

He couldn't look at her. The subject was too close to his heart, the pain too fresh, too vivid. *I do love you,* he thought, hoping his eyes would speak loud because the words would not come.

"What's going on Garrett? What did Lester say?"

Garrett drew in a deep breath, then exhaled slowly. His chest tightened. "He said he planned on tearing the house down."

Paige gasped. "Garrett, I'm not going to tell you what to do. You know how I feel about the mansion, and Granny. But I wish you'd be honest with me."

His brows drew together. "I am being honest with you."

Shaking her head, she said, "You're selling your grand-father's home for some other reason than what you've let on. Talk to me. Maybe I can help."

He forced a breath out, then pushed to his feet, paced to the window, and pushed the curtain aside to stare out. With his back to her, he said, "You're right. There is another reason why I'm selling the place." A long moment lingered before he turned to face her. "I thought I was protecting my mother, but I was only protecting myself."

She remained silent, allowing him to continue. He had a hard time meeting her stare, even though her eyes were filled with concern. He lifted his shoulders. "The mansion was the only tie she had left with this town." Garrett tried to summon the courage to confess the rest, admit about his past. How would Paige react? He had never told anyone his darkest secret before. He dipped his chin.

"Because you were taken from your parents' home?" Paige said it more as a statement than a question.

Garrett jerked his head up. She knew. Just as his mother had said.

"Garrett," Paige said, rising to her feet and crossing the room over to him.

The gentleness in her voice touched something deep inside him. He could trust her. He couldn't say that about many people.

"Every family has their share of problems. You don't

have to be perfect. Not anymore. Not with me. Especially with me." She wrapped her arms around him. "Don't you see? It's the flaws in people that make them unique, make them who they are."

Garrett held her tightly, never wanting to let go. He dropped a kiss on the side of her head. In a whisper he said, "You're one in a million."

"And don't forget it," Paige said, teasingly.

They stood there in each other's arms not speaking a word. This was exactly the type of support Garrett not only wanted, but needed from Paige. Garrett felt as if a heavy, almost unbearable load had fallen from his shoulders.

He had carried the burden of that secret for so long, and now, Paige knew, and no one could have understood better. After everything he had put her through, and every harsh word and accusation he had said about her and her family, she was still here with him, lending him comfort.

Garrett had to make it up to Paige, and there was only one way to do that—find the urn. And prove—he swallowed—Granny's innocence.

"I'm not going to sell the mansion. And the museum can stay where it's at, along with your ornery grandmother."

She took a step back, and gazed into his face. "I don't know what to say." Her words came out in a whisper. "Are you doing this for me?"

He stared into her eyes, and had never felt more in love with her than he did at that moment. He would die for her. As corny as that sounded, he would die for her. "I'm doing it for us."

"Oh, Garrett." She threw her arms around his neck and kissed him hard on the lips. Pulling back, she said, "I can't wait to tell Granny." She entwined her fingers with his. "Come on. Let's go tell her."

Garrett held his ground. "Why don't you go alone?"

"No. We should go together."

He shook his head. "We shouldn't go at all."

Paige frowned. "Why?"

Shifting his mind back into gear, Garrett said, "Because we first need to find the thief. If the urn theft and hauntings were connected to the sale of the mansion, then announcing our news might hurt our chances of ever catching the person behind all of this."

"Ah," she said, nodding. "You're right." Paige made a face. "It's sure going to be hard not telling Granny."

"Well, if it is Granny behind all of this, then she's gone to a lot of trouble for nothing."

"And if it isn't Granny," Paige said, "then what she doesn't know won't hurt her. At least for now."

The following morning, Garrett knocked on Granny's apartment door. Last night he had missed Paige. He wished she could be with him every night, but Paige didn't want to upset Granny. Besides, he was already on the old woman's bad list. To keep the peace he lived with the situation, and longed for the day when Paige would be beside him in bed every morning, every night, and once in awhile during the day.

Granny whisked the door open, a sneer instantly forming at the sight of him. "What do you want?"

"May I speak with Paige, please?"

Granny stood there as if debating whether she would allow it or not, her upper lip twitching.

"Who's at the door?" Paige asked.

With something between a grumble and a growl, Granny walked away, leaving Garrett feeling like an unwelcome visitor. Paige stepped over to the door.

"Come on," Garrett said.

"Where we going?"

"It's a surprise. Bring your coat and camera equipment."

Minutes later, Paige was riding in Garrett's truck, heading east on Main Street on a crisp, sunny Saturday morning.

"Close your eyes," Garrett said.

Paige never was good at following directions when she couldn't see where she was going so she peeked out the window now and then. "Where are we going?" Paige asked, acting like a curious cat.

"You'll see." They hadn't driven very far before Garrett said, "Okay. Open your eyes."

Paige could only stare at the inflated balloon, waiting for them in a the middle of an isolated grassy field located next to the Butler brothers' wrecking yard. "You've got to be kidding. Do you really expect me to get back into that thing?"

"Yes." Garrett hopped out of the truck and came around, opening her door. He extended his hand to her, and he had to tug on her arm to coax her out. He guided her over to the balloon. The Butler brothers were waiting for them.

"You told me to bring my camera equipment," Paige said.

"You never finished taking pictures of the town," Garrett said. "I wanted to help you."

Her heart warmed. How could it not? Garrett was making an effort to support her career, and be involved with her life. "Okay." She glanced at the Butler brothers holding the line. "I hope they intend to come with us this time."

"Don't worry," Moe said. "That'll never happen again." He climbed inside before Garrett did.

With effort, Paige suppressed her mounting anxiety. Her first experience in a hot air balloon turned out fine, but the

entire trip was harrowing. She didn't want to go through
that again. Garrett helped her into the gondola. Once inside,
she clung to the side of the basket.

Moe and his brothers took care of everything, from
checking the meters and releasing the ropes, to getting them
air borne, easily and smoothly.

Paige couldn't have asked for a better day. The air was
crisp and clean, and the sun shined in a brilliant, almost
cloudless blue sky. The storm had knocked off most of the
leaves, allowing Paige to focus more on the buildings and
people than the fall foliage. She attached the zoom lens to
her camera, then began snapping pictures. They floated
over the town, a slight breeze directing their course.

Between the company and scenery, Paige couldn't recall
a time when she felt more relaxed. All thoughts of the urn,
thief, and haunted mansion slipped away—at least for
awhile.

Garrett, bundled in a warm thick coat, stood next to her
in a comfortable quiet. They had no need for conversation.
Just being together was enough. His cheeks and nose were
red from the cold air, his hair was a bit disheveled, and his
face was closely shaven. To Paige he had never looked
more handsome.

As they drifted over the town, Paige focused the lens and
clicked picture after picture. She pointed the camera at City
Hall, the hardware store, and Mabel's Diner. Then she widened the angle, getting a snapshot of Main Street. She was
in her element taking photographs. Nothing made her happier, more content—until now. She glanced at Garrett and
smiled.

Bringing her attention back to the town, she focused on
the mansion coming up. "Garrett, someone just turned up
your driveway."

"It looks like Lester's car."

Paige felt a knot form in the pit of her stomach. Even though she believed Garrett wouldn't go back on his word when it came to selling the mansion, she still wasn't certain. After all, Garrett hadn't told Lester the deal was off. And time was running out. The thirty-day agreement between Garrett and Granny was over tomorrow.

"Were you expecting him?" Paige asked.

"No." Frown lines appeared on Garrett's forehead and around his eyes. His profile reminded Paige of Rocky, the way he narrowed his stare, the way his brows nearly touched, and the way his jaw slightly protruded when he was contemplating something.

"What are you thinking?" she asked.

He jerked his head toward her. "Nothing."

Garrett sure couldn't lie well, but Paige decided not to push the matter. Today was too perfect, being with a dashingly handsome man with whom she was in love, and he with her. Paige turned her attention to the other side of the street, clicking a string of shots.

"Paige," Garrett said. "Look."

The urgent tone of his voice made her turn quickly, then follow his gaze to the mansion. Lester dashed off the front porch, jumped in his sedan, and roared away.

As they floated closer to the mansion they heard the piano playing.

"I thought I gave you the remote," Paige said.

"You did. And I kept it at home."

"In the mansion?"

Garrett shook his head. "No. At the farmhouse I'm renting. Which means . . ."

When he fell silent Paige finished the thought for him. "Someone broke into your house and stole the remote."

"Unless someone's in there playing the piano."

Paige shook her head. "Someone's in there, all right, and doing their best to scare the contractor out of his wits. I wonder if something else happened? Lester sure took off in a hurry."

"I hear it's your grandpa's ghost," Moe said.

Garrett ignored Moe's comment. "When you're finished taking pictures, we'll investigate." He didn't seem very anxious to check out this turn of events. Did he just not care? Or did he suspect something—or someone?

Paige decided to take the same approach, and for the next hour she enjoyed the company and the scenery. At long last, she said, "I'm finished. I think I have enough pictures."

Garrett motioned to Moe to take the balloon down. He remained quiet the rest of the way, not saying a word until they landed in a vacant field. Moe's brothers were waiting, and one had brought Garrett's truck. Garrett discussed the balloon with them while Paige removed her equipment. Then the Butler brothers took over, deflating the balloon. Paige was amazed at how efficient and capable the Butlers were—this time.

Garrett took the scenic route back to his farm house and parked the car in the gravel driveway. "Would you like to come in?"

"Sure."

They entered into a family room through a sliding glass door on the side of the house. Paige hadn't expected the inside of Garrett's house to look like a zoo: Dogs and cats rested in cages, some sleeping, others barking or meowing. Bird cages hung from hooks screwed into the ceiling. An iguana crawled around in a large glass aquarium.

"Welcome to my humble home," Garrett said.

"Maybe I should call you Dr. Doolittle." Paige laughed, and rubbed a kitty through the wire bars on the cage.

He glanced at her and smiled. "It's part of the job. Most of these animals came from my mother's friends." He neglected to say those friends didn't have the means to pay for veterinary care, most on fixed retirement incomes.

Paige watched Garrett check on an older black dog with a cast on its front leg. She admired the gentle way he handled the animals, and knew from experience just how tender and gentle his hands could be. "May I help?" Paige asked.

His brows shot up, then relaxed. "Sure." He handed her a basset hound puppy. "His name's Harold," Garrett said.

"Harold?" Paige laughed. "What a silly name for a puppy with such a cute face."

"He looks much better," Garrett said. "Someone found him on the side of the road, cold, and near death."

"How could someone do that to an innocent and helpless animal?" She rubbed her cheek on his head. The puppy licked her nose, causing Paige to giggle. "That tickles."

"What else tickles you?" Garrett asked.

She met his eyes, and immediately spotted the desire in them.

"There's something about working with animals that brings out the animal in me," Garrett said, his voice thick and husky. He pulled her into him, the puppy between them. He lowered his mouth, capturing her lips. With an active tongue, the puppy licked Garrett's chin, then turned to Paige's, slopped a wet tongue on her cheek, and whimpered.

Paige giggled. "I've never been kissed by two males at once before."

Garrett took a step away, a grin creasing his lips—lips

that could heat her so quickly, so efficiently, so expertly. "I guess I should get back to work." He took Harold from her and set him back in his pen. The puppy's cries turned into howls.

"Should I hold him again?" Paige asked.

"No. He'll be fine." While Garrett attended to the animals, Paige wandered the room, then sat behind a desk, which turned out to be the only available chair in the room. "Do you have someone who does your office work?"

"My mother helps out, but I don't have a practice here. So I really don't have too much paper work, other than records for each of the animals."

Paige nodded, even though Garrett's back was to her. She looked around the room; it was nothing like the mansion. Instead, papers and files were spread everywhere, the desk and chair were hardly antique, and the room smelled of fur, feathers, and feed. More attention was clearly spent on the animals than the office.

Her glance halted on a sweater hanging on a coat rack near the back door. She got up to examine it more closely.

"Well, I'll be," Paige murmured.

"What?"

"Nothing." The pearl buttons on the sweater were just like the one she found in the music room. Just like the one she had accused her grandmother of losing. She counted the buttons. One was missing.

"Garrett," Paige said, trying to sound casual. "Whose sweater is this?"

Garrett gave a haphazard glance. "My mother's. Why?"

She shrugged. "No reason."

"You like it?" Despite his question, she could tell he wasn't paying attention to her or to the conversation. Just engaging in small talk. Paige did the same thing herself when working.

"Yes, it's nice." Paige's mind whirled with suspicion. Not once had Anne Taylor been a suspect, but shouldn't she be a prime candidate? She had opportunity, she knew the mansion inside and out, and Garrett would never be suspicious of her.

"Garrett, why doesn't your mother want you to sell the mansion?"

"I guess it's sentimental to her."

"Hmm." Paige returned to the desk and sat down, tapping her finger against her cheek in deep contemplation. "Does she know you don't intend to sell it?"

He paused momentarily to look at her. "No. I haven't told anyone except you. You know how fast news travels in this town."

Paige wondered what would happen if she just confronted Anne. She suspected Garrett would jump to her defense. "Garrett, have you ever thought your mother might be behind the hauntings and the robbery?"

She could hear the breath he forced out. "Yeah. Right. That's a good one."

Sitting up straighter in the chair, Paige said, "Why not?"

He moved to another cage before he glanced in her direction. "My mother do something like that? Come on. That's crazy. My mother's not the type."

"I didn't know there was a certain type of burglar."

Garrett turned towards her, and she could see the irritation in his frown. "Are you saying this because I think your grandmother is the prime suspect?"

"No. I'm just trying to look at all the possibilities."

"Well, you can forget about my mother. She'd never go

to all this trouble. And besides, what would her motive be for stealing the urn?"

Good point. Paige hadn't thought that one out yet. The phone rang, abruptly halting any further discussion on the subject.

Garrett snatched the receiver from its cradle. "Hello?" Paige listened to his one side of the conversation.

"Uh-huh . . . Are you sure?" After a few seconds, he hung up.

Paige waited for Garrett to say something. She could tell by the look on his face that something wasn't right.

When he remained silent she asked, "Is everything okay?"

"That was Lester. The deal's off. He said he doesn't want to buy a haunted house."

"I thought that's what you wanted," Paige said.

"I did. I just wanted to be the one who canceled the deal, not him."

"I guess that takes Lester out of the running for being the ghost."

Garrett smiled, but it was clearly a forced one. "I guess so."

The front door slammed shut, causing Garrett and Paige to turn and look. Anne came into the family room, removing her coat. "Did I hear you right?" she said. "The deal's off?"

The room became quiet enough to hear a pin drop.

"Don't worry, Mother. I'll sell the mansion."

She sighed loudly. Then, as if to emphasize her disgust, she plopped her purse on the floor next to the desk. "Why won't you give it up, Garrett? Keep the mansion. It's what your grandfather would have wanted."

"What would I do with it?"

"Live in it. Raise a family in it. Give tours of it in the summer. There's lots of things you could do with it." She opened Harold's cage and lifted him out, cuddling the puppy in her arms. "And how are we today?"

Paige cleared her throat and pushed out of the chair. "I need to get back to town, Garrett, and help Granny."

He readily nodded, relieved that he had somewhere to go. He helped her on with her coat, and whisked her outside.

Paige hardly had time to say goodbye to Anne, and remained quiet on the ride back to town.

When Garrett parked in front of the museum, he asked, "Would you like to go out for dinner tonight? We could drive into Portland."

"Sure." She smiled, collected her camera gear, then waved, watching him back out and drive away. Her mind drifted to the conversation Garrett had just had with his mother. Garrett had lied to Anne about selling the mansion. Which told Paige that in Garrett's mind, his mother wasn't completely removed from being a suspect.

At this point, other than Lester, no one was.

Chapter Ten

Paige wasn't too disappointed when Garrett canceled their dinner date for that evening. She didn't mind the time alone. Besides, she still had a puzzle to solve. And Paige hated unsolved mysteries. Especially when this particular one was driving a wedge between her and Garrett.

When Granny's poker buddies showed up, Paige readily agreed to run to the all-night market and pick up potato chips and other junk food. The cigar smoke was thicker than ever tonight, almost suffocating Paige. For the past several weeks, on poker nights, she would escape Granny and her buddies and have a quiet evening alone with Garrett, staying with him until morning. Not tonight. One of Garrett's animal patients had taken a turn for the worse, and he needed to stay with the sick animal.

Paige admired his dedication. She loved animals, too, especially cats. In fact, she had planned on sleeping in front of a warm fire in the parlor with her own fur ball tonight.

Buster had made himself a permanent fixture in the mansion, and from the look of it, he didn't intend to change his residence any time soon.

After dropping off Granny's goodies, Paige ventured into the mansion, carrying a burger, fries and shake, not to mention a can of cat food for Buster. A cozy fire warmed the parlor, bringing a smile to Paige's lips, and a warmth to her heart at Garrett's thoughtfulness. He'd remembered tonight was Granny's poker night, and that Paige would be coming here. She hoped he could join her later.

Looking like a dead rug, Buster was stretched out on the sofa—he had claimed it as his own—deep in sleep. He barely looked up when Paige entered the room and sat down across from him.

Paige propped her feet on the coffee table and stared into the fire while she ate her burger and fries. Two things occupied her mind these days: Garrett and the mystery. Over and over she mentally went through the list of suspects. Granny did have the strongest motive. And Paige could see Granny haunting the house, but she couldn't be the thief. With Granny's arthritis and the weight of the urn, it was impossible for Granny to have stolen it. On the other hand, any of her friends could have done it for her.

The other suspects on the list were Anne Taylor and Jeannie. Unless she was overlooking the obvious—could it be Garrett himself?

From what sounded like it was coming from the kitchen, Paige heard a door click shut. She held her breath, waiting for footsteps to come toward her, but none did.

Buster jerked his head up and stared at the hallway leading to the parlor.

"Garrett? Is that you?"

Dead silence followed.

All Paige heard was the sound of her breath, and her heart pounding in her chest.

Now suddenly alert, Buster darted off the sofa and scrambled out of the room. He took a sharp right.

"Where are you going, Buster?" Paige followed Buster's path into the foyer, looked around, then continued into the kitchen. She found Buster sniffing his food bowl.

She glanced out the window. The moonlight, partially hidden behind the tall fir trees, didn't allow for much of a view. The only other light that offered any help came from Granny's apartment, but it was too far away to be much help.

Movement near the edge of the woods caught Paige's attention. Was it a tree branch or bush swaying in the wind? Paige shook her head. Her imagination was running wild. That's all.

She started to turn when she saw a beam of light flickering through the trees. On second thought, it wasn't her imagination. Was this person the one who was in the house? Could this be her ghost?

She rushed into the parlor, grabbed her coat, and slipped it on as she made her way out of the kitchen door. Suddenly it occurred to her that the person in the woods could very well be Booker, going to get another jug of moonshine.

Her first stop was Granny's apartment. She ducked her head in the door, barely getting a glance from the group at the table. Everyone was present and accounted for. Grabbing a flashlight, Paige hastened outside, striding to the edge of the woods. The towering trees engulfed her in total darkness. She slowed her pace.

The path wasn't as clear now as compared to the daytime, and debris still covered parts of the trail.

She ended up, as she knew she would, at Jeannie's

house. Shining the light on the garage, she noticed a large gap between the driveway and the bottom of the garage door.

Paige crouched down, and quietly raised the garage door. She searched for a light switch on the wall, found it, and flipped it on. Now the garage was empty, except for a wheelbarrow in the center of the floor.

She sucked in a sharp breath. Sitting upright in the wheelbarrow was the urn. Paige glanced over her shoulder. An eerie feeling that someone was watching came over her.

"Grandpa you're not getting away from me this time," Paige said aloud. Grasping the handles of the wheelbarrow, she pushed it out of the garage and back on the path. The going wasn't easy as she tried to maneuver the wheelbarrow while keeping the flashlight on the path.

A light perspiration coated her body by the time she reached Granny's apartment. She opened the door and said, "Come out here. I have something you need to see." The tone in her voice left no room for argument.

Granny and the gang stomped to the door. Outside, they surrounded the wheelbarrow, their mouths wide open.

"Ta-da!" Paige said, spreading her arms wide. "And for my next trick I'll make the urn disappear!"

"You're not saying you're behind this, are you?" Granny asked.

"Of course I'm not. But I've found this darn thing before and it's disappeared on me. This time I think we should keep it somewhere safe where no one can steal it."

"I've got the perfect place," Booker said.

"Where?" Paige asked.

"The jailhouse." Picking up the urn, Booker led the procession over to the sheriff's office.

Sheriff Raymond glanced up, a bit surprised to see

Granny and her poker buddies at his door this late in the evening. "What do we have here?"

"The urn," they said in unison.

"Paige found it," Granny said.

Sheriff Raymond focused his stare on Paige. "You did? Where'd you find it?"

"In Jeannie Nelson's garage."

Sheriff Raymond just nodded, then lifted the phone.

"Who you calling?" Booker asked.

"Jeannie Nelson." When the sheriff didn't get an answer, he hung up the phone and dialed another number. "Well, let's try Garrett Taylor."

Only a few words were exchanged before he hung the phone up. "He's on his way."

Paige wondered if Garrett coming was a good thing, or a bad thing.

Garrett brought his truck to an abrupt halt in front of the sheriff's office. He burst through the door, making eye contact with Paige, then he saw the urn, sitting on the sheriff's desk. He maneuvered around the group until he stood next to Paige, his hand automatically folding around the curve of her waist. He had missed being with her tonight, their night. The scent of her perfume, and the fullness of her lips warmed him through and through.

He gave her a reassuring squeeze, followed by a smile. "This is great news."

"It won't be when you hear where I found it," Paige said.

Garrett frowned, then waited for her to finish.

"In Jeannie's garage." She had an accusing tone in her voice, as if to say, "I-told-you-so."

Garrett wasn't defensive as he knew Jeannie had nothing to do with the situation. "Jeannie's out of town."

"Maybe that's what she wants you to think," Granny said.

Just the old woman's voice was enough to get Garrett's ire up. "Do you want me to prove it?"

"Maybe you should," Booker said.

Garrett flipped out his wallet and dug for the card on which Jeannie had written the number where she was be staying. He dialed the long distance phone number.

"Jeannie, this is Garrett."

"Garrett, is something wrong? Is my house okay?"

"Everything's fine—except—" How was he supposed to say this?

"Except what?"

"Except the urn that was stolen from the museum was just found in your garage."

A lengthy silence followed on the line.

"I don't know how it could have gotten there," Jeannie said. "I've been out of town for a week. You saw the garage before I left."

"I know. I just wanted you to tell the sheriff that." He handed Sheriff Raymond the phone.

The sheriff mumbled a few questions, then hung up. "Well, it looks like Jeannie Nelson couldn't be the thief. She's been out of town for over a week. She's given me the names and numbers of people who could verify her story."

"The urn could have been there for that length of time," Lily said.

" 'O what a goodly outside falsehood hath!' " Jean said.

"No." Paige said. "I saw someone in the woods heading for Jeannie's. That's why I went there in the first place."

"We thought you should keep the urn here, Sheriff," Booker said. "Just until things calm down a bit."

"And until we can get better security in the museum," Granny said, glaring over at Garrett as if that was his responsibility.

"I'll lock it up for safekeeping," Sheriff Raymond said. "Now, why don't you all go home? Deputy Dave and I will investigate tomorrow when there's more light. I'll make some phone calls to check out Jeannie's story. There's nothing more I can do for you tonight."

Reluctantly, the group moseyed out the door, chatting anxiously about the urn.

Garrett remained behind. Once everyone left, he said, "I'd like you to check for fingerprints on the urn. And let me know as soon as possible."

Sheriff Raymond held Garrett's stare for several long seconds before he nodded and said, "Will do."

"Thanks, Sheriff."

Garrett made a hasty exit and found Paige leaning her backside against his truck.

"What were you doing?" she asked.

"I'll tell you later." He slid his arm across her shoulders. "It's freezing out here. Let's get you home and in front of a warm fire."

"Are you joining me?"

How could he resist? "You bet."

Back at the mansion, Paige nestled in Garrett's arms on the sofa in the parlor. They remained quiet, staring into the flames dancing in the fireplace. At long last, Paige said, "I guess this proves Granny had nothing to do with the robbery."

Garrett said, "I guess so."

"I told you you were wrong about her."

"Maybe."

She turned her head to look at him. "What do you mean, 'maybe'?"

"We still don't know if the person who stole the urn is the same person haunting the house."

"True." She fell back into his arms and rested her head against his chest, listening to the rhythm of his heartbeat. "And, really, we were just speculating on the two being connected in the first place."

"Which means if they aren't connected, then Granny could still be the one haunting the house." His hand unconsciously tightened on her arm.

Buster strolled into the parlor, jumped on the sofa, and curled himself on Paige's lap. She stroked his fluffy white fur and he began to purr.

"I guess it doesn't matter who was haunting the house, now that you're not going to sell it," Paige said.

"It matters to me."

"Why?"

"Because I want to know how and why this person was doing it. If we intend to live here and raise a family, we need to know who knows this house's secrets better than we do."

"We intend to live here and raise a family, huh?" Paige asked.

Garrett's smile wavered. "That is, if it's okay with you. We might as well get some use out of the place. Besides, we've already started."

"What are you talking about?" Paige asked.

Garrett scratched Buster's head. "With this little guy here."

Paige's heart warmed. "And let's not forget Harold."

"I didn't know we were going to keep the puppy," Garrett said.

"I think Buster needs a brother, don't you?"

"Buster can have whatever he wants since he brought us together."

"How so?" Paige asked.

"Well, if he hadn't come into the mansion when he did, and you hadn't come looking for him when you did, I would never have kissed you. And that's all it took, just one kiss and I knew you were the only one for me," Garrett said.

Paige kissed him, then returned her attention to petting Buster. "But what about the farmhouse?"

"I'll keep using it as a clinic until I find another place or build a new one."

Things were getting serious. Paige waited for the panic to set in, but it never came. Instead, a feeling of rightness came over her. A sense that they belonged together, no matter the circumstance, no matter their backgrounds. Fate had brought them together. And, God willing, nothing would tear them apart. Not Granny. Not the haunted house. Not the urn.

At long last, Paige felt as if she had truly come home. Patterson used to be a nightmare for her, years of painful memories. Now she could build a life here with Garrett, beginning new, happy memories for them and their children.

And what about her career? She knew Garrett would never stand in her way, and she was more than ready for a change. She would be moving into the career of motherhood. Her biological clock had been telling her it was ready for the past year, but ignoring it had been easy to do because she lacked a key ingredient in her life—a husband.

Now she had found a wonderful man with whom she could be happy, a man that would love her for just being her. Suddenly, she felt free, liberated from the constraints of people's past prejudices. What did it matter what anyone thought of her? She was Paige McCormick, and yes, her father made mistakes, big ones that hurt a lot of people. If anyone judged her by that, then they weren't worth knowing.

She could hold her head high because she was a good person; caring, loving, giving—and so tired of running from her past. Soon her name would be Paige Taylor. A smile crossed her lips. She liked the sound of it.

"What are you thinking?" Garrett asked.

"About us."

"All good, I hope." He kissed the top of her head. "I've searched my whole life for someone like you."

He chuckled.

"What?"

"You know I really have to love you in order for me to put up with your grandmother."

"And I really must love you to put up with living in a haunted house."

"Are we going to start with that again?"

"Well, you know, Garrett, we don't really have any proof this house isn't haunted."

"Sure we do. We have the remote that turned the piano on and off."

"Did you ever find the remote?" Paige asked.

"Nope."

"Are you sure it was in your house?"

"Yes. I put it in my tool box, thinking that that was a safe place for it, and then I forgot about it. Later, I couldn't find it."

"Maybe you misplaced it."

"I don't think so."

"And since you took that toolbox back and forth between here and your farm house, anyone could have taken it," Paige said.

"Including someone walking by when I was at the hardware store," Garrett added.

"Which brings us back to square one, again."

He patted her arm and nuzzled his lips near her ear. "Don't worry, we'll know soon enough."

"Why do you say that?"

"Because I asked the sheriff to take fingerprints off the urn."

Paige smacked the palm of her hand against her forehead. "You know what? I forgot to look inside to see if Grandpa was still there."

"We can check tomorrow. Soon this whole mystery will be solved. And—" He kissed her neck. "You and I—" He nibbled her earlobe. "Can get on with our lives." To finish his statement he kissed her, deepening the kiss quickly and without warning.

When he lifted his head, he said, "I like your grandmother's poker nights."

The next day, Garrett had gone to the museum early. He'd asked each possible suspect to meet him here. Before they came, he placed the urn back onto its stand, then replaced its glass case.

Granny, Paige, Booker, Vivian, Lily, Jean, Sheriff Raymond, Deputy Dave, and Anne arrived within minutes of each another. They stood next to the urn and waited for Garrett to begin.

"I've gathered all of you here today to once and for all

solve the mystery of who stole the urn, and perhaps, the haunted house. Because I suspect the two are connected."

His gaze passed from person to person. No one seemed to squirm or become uncomfortable. "I asked Sheriff Raymond to take fingerprints off of the urn."

"That's not fair," Granny said. "I put my husband in the urn. My prints will be all over it."

"I know that, and rest assured, your husband is safe and sound inside," Garrett said.

Granny relaxed the worry lines on her forehead.

Garrett's gaze slipped to Paige.

She smiled.

"For a long time, Granny, I suspected you were haunting the house, but Paige convinced me that you wouldn't have stolen the urn no matter how much insurance money you thought you might get."

"That's right." Granny nodded. "It's about time you came to your senses and listened to reason."

Ignoring the barb, Garrett continued. "Booker's prints were on the urn along with one other set." He decided to prolong the suspense. "For awhile, I suspected Booker. Not only did he have a motive, but he had the strength to lift the urn and carry it away. But then it showed up in my grandparents' bedroom, and I realized it had to have been stolen by someone who had access to my home, and who knew the ins and outs of the mansion."

Now mentioning the mansion as his home sounded right, and pride filled him.

"How much longer are you going to drag this out?" Granny mumbled.

Staring at the old woman, Garrett said, "Then, I suspected it could be any one of Granny's friends, or all of them."

"What about your cousin, Jeannie?" Booker asked.

"Paige thought it was Jeannie the entire time. But Jeannie's an antique dealer and doesn't have the time to spend haunting a house. Besides, what would she have had to gain from it?"

"How do you know someone was haunting the house?" Granny said. "It could very well be your grandfather trying to get through your thick skull that he doesn't want the place sold."

Garrett folded his arms over his chest. "Because Paige found a remote that turns the player piano on and off."

"That's true," Booker added. "A few years back, Rocky had me make him a remote for the piano; his arthritis had gotten so bad he couldn't play it any more. So I tinkered around and got a remote to work for him."

"What about the sightings of Rocky in the mansion?" Lily asked.

Garrett shrugged. "Sightings of what? Windows opened, floor boards creaked, silhouettes appeared against curtains, making people think they were seeing the ghost of my grandfather. But did anyone actually see Rocky?"

He surveyed the group. They all shook their heads.

"The night of the Halloween dance, Booker said he saw Rocky through the window," Garrett said.

All eyes focused on Booker. Booker became slightly flustered. "I saw someone moving in the rooms, but I didn't actually see Rocky."

"What about the footsteps and banging noises I heard in the house all the time?" Granny asked, in a challenging manner.

"I believe you did hear someone walking around the house," Garrett said. "Which brings me back to the fact that the person who was haunting the house had to know it inside and out. And there's only one person who knows the mansion better than I do. And that person's fingerprints also happen to be on the urn."

Garrett turned towards Anne. "That person is my mother."

Everyone in the group gasped as they turned to look at her.

Anne's face flushed. She folded her arms over her chest. "Okay, I admit it. I stole the urn, and haunted the house."

"Why?" Granny asked.

Anne's glance dropped to the floor before she looked back at Granny. "I'm sorry. I never meant to hurt any of you. I just didn't want my son to sell the mansion." She took a deep breath. "Years ago, Garrett's grandparents took him in. They were there for him when no one else was. They helped him get through those ugly times, giving him things his father was incapable of, like love, acceptance, and self-esteem. I wanted to give something back to Rocky and Gretta—and that was to save their mansion. I knew how much this house meant to Rocky. When Garrett was so determined to sell it, I knew I had to do something."

Tears glistened in her eyes. She drew another deep breath, exhaling in a rush. "So I started to haunt the mansion in hopes that no one would buy the place. But my son—the stubborn man he is—refused to give up. I knew Granny loved the museum as much as I loved the mansion, and would do whatever it took to save it. I thought that if I stole the urn, she could collect the insurance from it and buy the mansion."

She forced a smile, her eyes pleading for Granny's forgiveness. "Then, one day when I was in here, I overheard you tell Paige that the insurance wouldn't pay up. So I increased my efforts to haunt the mansion."

"What about when I found the urn in the closet?" Paige asked.

"The day I stole it, I hid it in Jeannie's garage until it was safe to move. Then I hid it in the mansion. It's been there most of the time. I had to keep moving it around because Garrett kept working on different parts of the house."

A hush fell over the room.

"I'm very sorry about everything," Anne said.

"I think your son should be the one who's sorry," Granny said. "Look what you've put your mother through."

Sheriff Raymond cleared his throat. "I hate to do this, Anne, but I'm going to have to arrest you."

"What for?" Granny demanded.

Everyone in the group angrily glared at the sheriff.

"For robbery," Sheriff Raymond replied.

"She didn't steal anything," Granny said. "I—uh—loaned her the urn."

Booker rubbed his jaw. "Yes. I recall Granny doing that. Anne borrowed the urn. And that's not against the law, is it, Sheriff?"

"And there's no law against haunting a house," Lily said. "Right, Sheriff?"

Sheriff Raymond sighed, raising his hands in surrender. "Okay, you win. But she will have to pay for damages to the museum."

"I'll pay for those," Garrett said.

Deputy Dave stepped forward, yanking his britches up. "I knew it all along. I knew the mansion wasn't haunted." He tapped his temple. "It's this keen intuition I have for solving crimes."

Patting Deputy Dave on the shoulder, Sheriff Raymond

said, "Come on, Dave. Let's go." They ambled out of the museum.

"What I want to know is if you intend to keep your promise and let the museum remain here?" Granny asked. "The thirty days are up today, and the museum did turn a profit."

"Yes, what do you intend to do now, son?" Anne asked.

All eyes were on Garrett. He positioned himself next to Paige and slid his arm around her shoulders. "I intend to live in the mansion with my soon-to-be wife. And the museum can stay here for as long as Granny likes. Unless she wants to give us an early wedding present and move herself and the museum somewhere else." He raised his brow, goading the old woman.

"Over my dead body," Granny said.

Garrett mocked a frown. "I figured as much."

"But I will provide the moonshine at the wedding reception," Granny said. The group cheered.

"And I'll give the bride away," Booker said.

Vivian clapped her hands. "I'll make the wedding dress."

"What about the flowers?" Jean asked. " 'I know a bank where the wild thyme blows, Where oxslips and the nodding violet grows, Quite over-canopied with luscious woodbine, With sweet musk-roses and with eglantine.' "

"Shakespeare's *A Midsummer Night's Dream,*" the group said in unison.

Anne joined the group. "Can the mother of the groom do something to help?"

"Of course," Booker said. "We'll need food at the reception."

Granny, Anne, and the group ambled toward the exit, all talking excitedly about the upcoming wedding.

Garrett remained with Paige, turning her into his arms. "I can't wait until we're married."

"Me too."

"Looks like we'll both have outlaws for in-laws," Garrett said.

Paige laughed.

Suddenly, a loud crash came from inside the house.

Everyone froze, exchanging bewildered glances.

Paige and Garrett simultaneously said, "Buster!"